OUT OF THE RAIN

OUT OF THE RAIN

A Novel

J. MALCOLM GARCIA

Seven Stories Press

New York · Oakland · London

Some of the chapters in this work were originally published in the *Alaska Quarterly Review, Bull, Green Hills Literary Lantern, McSweeney's, River Oak Review*, War, Literature & the Arts, and *Zyzzyva*.

Seven Stories Press
140 Watts Street
New York, NY 10013
www.sevenstories.com

Library of Congress Cataloging-in-Publication Data

[tk]

College professors and high school and middle school teachers may order free examination copies of Seven Stories Press titles. Visit https://www.sevenstories.com/pg/resources-academics or email academic@sevenstories.com.

Printed in the United States of America

9 8 7 6 5 4 3 2 1

for Sandy Weiner

When you're strange
Faces come out of the rain
When you're strange
No one remembers your name
When you're strange
When you're strange
When you're strange

"People Are Strange"
THE DOORS

Tom

I'm standing at Golden Gate and Leavenworth across from Fresh Start. It's a program that serves the homeless in the Tenderloin. I'm the director, I'm in charge, but not really. What happens on a given day more often ends up directing me than the other way around. We offer twenty-four-hour detox and a daytime drop-in center. In another building on Leavenworth we have a homeless shelter. I have four floor supervisors, six counselors, a benefits advocate, an outreach worker, and two support group facilitators. Homeless men and women also help out as volunteers. They mop the floors, check people in at the front desk, answer phones, serve snacks, and make coffee. In exchange, I guarantee them a shelter bed.

Glancing up at the second-floor window of my office, I see my boss, James McGraw, leaning over my desk. What's he doing here? Squinting through the gray morning fog, I watch him open a cabinet and remove a file. I rub my face, look at the time on my phone. Eight o'clock. He never comes in this early, and he has never riffled through my files, at least that I know of. Sure, he's the executive director. He can do what he wants, but I don't like this. More than that, I know it can't be good.

I open and close my eyes, open and close them again, and shake my head. My temples pound with the reverb of a hangover. I take a deep breath and try to shake it off knowing that's not going to work. You knock off a six-pack of Budweiser the night before and this is what happens, I tell myself. Should've taken two or three Advil when I got up this morning. Could've used some coffee too. Rather have a beer to take the edge off, for real. Might have one for lunch then stop somewhere for a grilled cheese sandwich with onions and garlic to kill my breath. Learned that trick from Walter, a forty-something homeless alcoholic. I've put Walter in detox more than a few times. One day he came in slurring his words and swaying, and I noticed that I didn't smell booze on his breath. It was godawful in every way, thick enough to cut with a knife, heavy with undefinable odor, but nothing I could discern as alcohol. I mentioned that to him and he told me in a rush of barely intelligible words about his grilled cheese sandwich concoction. He thought of it after our social worker got him a job interview at a temp agency. Walter had some time before the interview and started drinking. He knew he couldn't risk smelling like Thunderbird wine. So he went to David's Deli on Larkin Street and ordered a grilled cheese with a unique set of ingredients he thought would obscure the fact he'd been drinking. He winked at me, thought he was pretty clever. Then he asked for detox. When I saw him later, he never mentioned the interview, so I presume he didn't get the job. Being barely able to stand probably didn't score him any points, breath or no breath. He drank way too much for his sandwich trick to work. Lesson learned. One beer at lunch, I tell myself. One beer and a grilled cheese sandwich.

Moisture collects on my beard, the fog so dense it clings like an extra layer of clothes. A shiver rattles my spine. I expect the fog won't lift until midday. Typical San Francisco winter. I should've called in sick with this hangover, then tried to persuade my girlfriend, Mary, to do the same and come over. She's a paralegal at Welfare Mother's United, an advocacy group for single moms. A few months ago, her boss asked me to speak to her staff about what we do at Fresh Start. I noticed Mary right off. She had curly black hair and a smile that pulled me in faster than a whirlpool does a drowning man.

Are you coming over? she asked me last night. I was on my third beer by then.

I want to, I said, but I'm tired. I think I'll stay in.

There was a long pause before she said, OK.

I felt sort of bad. Then I drained my beer and got up for another one.

It had been a bad day. I fired one of my staff, a guy named Frank Harrison. When I hired him, Frank had just graduated from a forty-five-day alcoholism program and had moved out of a halfway house and into a hotel for recovering drunks on Ellis Street. Then he came in loaded one day for his shift and I told him to leave. Had he left, eventually we could have worked something out. I would've cut him a deal: You can keep your job if you stop drinking and attend at least one AA meeting a day, but he didn't leave. He cussed me out and threw a vase of fake flowers at my head, clipping my left ear. A little more to the right and I would have had a full-on concussion. I can handle being cussed out; a broken head, not so much. I cut him loose. But I was generous. I mean, I've got a heart. If I fired him, I knew he wouldn't be eligible for unemployment. However, if I called his termination a layoff, he would be. A layoff isn't an employee's fault. I had nothing against Frank. He just started drinking again. Most of my staff does. I drink, but I don't act a fool at work. There's a difference.

Frank didn't act particularly appreciative. In fact, he didn't say anything, I mean literally not a word. He just left. Like everything had gone according to plan, as if he had planned for this outcome. No job, no reason to stop drinking. I felt set up in a way. He didn't need an excuse but I gave him one. And I guess he gave me one too, because I knew he'd be one more of my guys I'd see back on the street. It's not my fault, but it weighs heavy. Or maybe like Frank, I just wanted to drink too. Whatever. I sure tied one on last night.

What's going on, Tom Murray?

I turn to see Walter walking up behind me.

Morning, Walt. I was just thinking of you.

What about?

Nothing special.

He tugs a blue cloth cap down on his head; a storm of gray curls sprouts out around both of his ears. When he doesn't wear the cap, he sports a toupee so black it looks like he shined it with shoe polish. The hairpiece slants increasingly askew as the day and his level of intoxication progress.

This morning, his hands shake as violently as my head is pounding. A rip stretches like a scar down a sleeve of his open brown corduroy jacket. He's wearing a couple of sweaters punched with holes. The breeze carries the odor of his sweat-dampened clothes into my face. He has a bird-lidded look, as if he is still half asleep.

What's going on, Tom Murray? he asks again.

Coming to work, same ol' same ol'.

You got circles under your eyes as big as hammocks.

I'm taking on the characteristics of my clients.

Walter laughs, revealing saliva-slick pink gums absent of teeth. He always calls me by my full name. Tom Murray, where're you going? Tom Murray, I need to talk to you. Tom Murray, what're you doing? Like a parent scolding me. He says he's from Gulfport, Mississippi. Lost his home in a hurricane and came to San Francisco because he has family in Oakland. I don't know if any of this is true, but if he has people across the Bay they must not want to see him, because I refer him to our shelter almost every night.

Tom Murray, help me out with a dollar.

A dollar? What're you going to get for a dollar?

I give him ten bucks and tell him to buy us both some coffee. He hurries up Leavenworth to a convenience store on Eddy. I don't expect him to buy coffee for either of us, not the way he's shaking. In a few days he'll pay me back. He's good about that. He'll hand me a ten-dollar bill, maybe more, whatever he thinks he owes, and I'll take it knowing I'll give it back to him in a day or two. But at that moment when I take the money from him he will smile and feel pretty good about himself. See Tom Murray, I told you I'd get it back to you, the grin on his face will declare, and it will be a genuine and honest expression of how he's feeling at that moment, not his shuck and jive, what-can-I-get-out-of-Tom-Murray routine. I will thank him and he'll feel part of the human race again, a guy like any other paying his debts, as if he owed a balance on a credit card. Or maybe not. Maybe he's just playing me for a fool he knows will give him more money the next time. I try not to give it too much thought.

You need a new coat, Walter. It's December, man, you'll freeze.

Clothes closet going to be open, Tom Murray?

Yeah, and if we don't have what you need, go to Sally's, I tell him, using the shorthand for Salvation Army.

Mr. McGraw's in your office, Tom Murray.

I see that.

I saw him go in.

What time?

Maybe an hour ago.

Seven o'clock in the morning?

Walter shrugged.

You in trouble, Tom Murray?

No more than usual, I don't think.

Walter laughs.

You want cream in your coffee, Tom Murray?

Sure.

I first met McGraw three years earlier at the monthly meeting of the Department of Social Services. The directors of nonprofit programs for the homeless always attended. Salvation Army, Episcopal Sanctuary, St. Vincent de Paul Society, the whole clique. They used their time to plead for money. I was a social worker for Central City Shelter on Ninth Street. The director, Harry Earl, would drag me along to talk about clients we had helped get jobs and housing.

I respect the difficulties the city faces with the budget, Harry began, always the diplomat. Still, I'd appreciate it if you would remember the numbers of people we've saved from the streets when you consider the budget. Whatever you do, we'll continue our work knowing we can count on your support.

After he finished, Harry would fold his hands and bow his head as if he was about to pray. He had a thick mustache and goatee that lent him the dignified air of a monk straight out of the Middle Ages. The twelve commissioners always thanked him for his good work. Harry would nudge me to start my spiel. I rattled off stories of guys finding work after years of being on the street. I didn't bother to say these were day labor jobs and that they took the work in the middle of the month after they'd gone through their general assistance checks and needed money for alcohol and drugs. No, I just talked about guys like Walter going to a warehouse to unload trucks for eight hours as if it was a new day dawning for the Seven Dwarfs: Heigh ho, heigh ho, it's off to work we go. Really, I made myself sick sometimes with my bullshit. We were begging and telling lies, but as long as we told the lies the commissioners wanted to hear, we'd get our money.

Then at one commission meeting, the secretary asked if James

McGraw with New Horizons Inc. had any comments. Harry groaned.

He's new, and he's trouble, Harry said.

New Horizons was a small agency that offered shelter to homeless people. McGraw, a former welfare-rights advocate, had just become executive director and had plans to expand. I'd heard his name mentioned at provider meetings, but I didn't know him. When I saw him at one of the monthly meetings, he was wearing a loud purple shirt and a thin, black leather tie. A bush of untamed blond hair spread in all directions like vines searching for a trellis. Hands on his right hip, a corner of his dark blue jacket draped behind him. His left fist gripped a piece of paper that he glanced at before he spoke. He looked furious. He didn't have to open his mouth for me to know he wasn't there to beg.

I wrote down my comments, but I don't need this, he said waving the paper. I don't have to remind myself of what to say, because I know it; I see it every day in our shelter when I come to work. We provide people with barely enough to rent a skid row hotel room a dog wouldn't live in, and you want to cut their checks even further so they can't afford even that, he said in a high pitched, nasal voice. We foundations appeal to the state for moneys it says it has and we get nothing but scraps, and we're expected to feel grateful.

His glasses crept down his nose and he scrunched his face to push them back up, tossing his head to keep one of many strands of hair from his eyes. He looked at his paper and then jammed it into his jacket pocket.

I never understood budgets and spreadsheets and why people said moneys when they talked about grants instead of just money. I got lost in the intricacies of community block grants and federal McKinney fund applications and in abbreviations: CMHS,

HUD, HA, TLSHC, HIC, and, of course, DSS. What I did understand was that there weren't enough shelter beds, weren't enough detoxes, weren't enough jobs, weren't enough anything for the people I wanted to help. Whenever I got someone a place to live, it was always in a filthy hotel room I'd never stay in. Listening to McGraw, I realized I wasn't alone. Maybe he understood why people said "moneys" instead of "money." Maybe he knew what all those abbreviations stood for. He probably did. But what mattered to me was that he sounded like he felt the same way I did about those crappy hotel rooms.

Imagine sleeping on a bed stained with dried urine and filled with lice, he said. Imagine scratching yourself. Imagine thinking that this is what your city feels you are worth. Now you want to take even that away. We don't have enough room in the shelters for the people coming to us at night. Where exactly would those people who now stay in hotels go when they can no longer afford their rooms? The turn-away figures for shelters are up twenty percent this year. Low-income housing stock has fallen ten percent. There's no fat on the bone. Never was. Perhaps we'll just refer our people to the front lawns of your homes, and you can provide them with the tents and sleeping gear you bought your children for their Boy Scout camping trips.

When he stopped talking, the commissioners stared at him looking as jittery as someone suffering from indigestion. Maybe they were. Thank you, the chairman finally said and closed the meeting. As we got out of our chairs, agency directors clustered around McGraw and talked at once. Jesus, what are you doing? Just promote your agency, they told him. Don't scold. We have to work with these people. They recommend our budgets to the Board of Supervisors. Are you trying to lose all your funding? McGraw smirked, turned, and walked away. I watched him leave. I thought, I want to be that guy.

I didn't get into social work for the love of people. I delivered pizzas for Charlie's Restaurant out in the Mission. I double-parked all the time and collected enough tickets to wallpaper a house. A judge sentenced me to one hundred hours of community service at Central City. I served coffee and put mats on the floor at night for the shelter. Every so often, I ripped off a few pizzas and donated them. After a few weeks, one of the shelter staff started drinking again and lost his job, and Harry offered the position to me. The job paid more than Charlie's. I took it.

My coworkers were all guys who had been homeless. They had drunk most of their lives away and hadn't worked in years before Harry hired them out of detox. They were nervous and seemed to think they were going to screw up. A lot of them started drinking again just to get the screw-up part over with rather than to keep waiting for it to happen. I did my job and didn't trip. In a couple of months, I was promoted to shift supervisor. Day after day, I made calls to find shelter for families when we had no room.

Nothing.

Day after day, I made calls to see which inpatient alcohol programs had beds.

Nothing.

Day after day, I called temp agencies to see who was hiring.

Nothing.

Day after day, I talked to every agency and asked for something

Day after day, what did I have to offer?

Nothing real.

I didn't have to love people to know this was wrong.

About two months after I had seen McGraw, Harry asked me to fill in for him at a DSS meeting. Just do what I do, he said, thank them for their support and that's it. But by then I was sick and tired of the hamster wheel entrapping our clients. Just the previous night I'd spoken to a guy who had completed an alcohol program. He was on the waiting list for a halfway house and needed shelter, but we had no space for him, and every other shelter was full too. I advised him to spend the night at a Denny's. It's open twenty-four seven. That counted as a housing referral and I put it down in my stats. Numbers don't lie, people do; and I was lying for a living. I just waited to clock out so I could go home and crack that first Bud. So when I stood before the commissioners, my heart thumping because I was not accustomed to speaking in front of people and was hungover to boot, I let loose my frustration.

Not only should you fund us, but you need to fund many more like us, I told the commissioners. We need more programs, not fewer. We have no place to refer people. My hands shook. I spoke too fast. I lost my place in my notes. I felt the blank, angry looks of the commissioners. I stopped talking and sank into my seat. McGraw leaned over.

Good job, dude, he said.

A few months later McGraw asked me to be the director of what he had dubbed his adult services initiative. This included three programs he had recently acquired through state and city grants: Fresh Start; The Bridge, a transitional housing program; and The McLeod, a hotel for homeless addicts. In addition, he had received funding to enlarge the homeless shelter at New Horizons.

I took the job and my name was soon added to a chart in his office of the new programs. Small squares held the names of individual staff members. From those boxes ran lines to other boxes that held the names of shift supervisors. Their boxes in turn connected to a box with my name. A rectangle at the top of the chart held McGraw's name in bold block letters. My box linked to his.

New Horizons was no longer a small agency. However, I would soon see how much McGraw's adult services initiative had cost him. To maintain his programs he needed to maintain the city's financial support. Once a month at the DSS meeting he had to court the same commissioners he had once mocked. They said nothing but offered McGraw thin smiles, expressing their contempt, I think, for his 180-degree turn. Maybe not. Maybe they smirked at all of us. McGraw may have been late to the party but we were all beggars. Whatever they thought of him, he was playing by their rules now and no longer railing against crappy hotel rooms. They gave him his money. Prodigal son. I don't remember how I felt. Betrayed sounds right. I mean what happened to the guy who stood up to the commissioners and said things I'd been thinking for a long time? How do you just turn like that and become someone else? He was no different from my old boss Harry. Maybe he just grew up. I get the money thing and all, but man. He was no bullshit. And then he was all bullshit, obedient as a guide dog. And so was I, because I didn't object. The money thing applied to me too. I had a job. I worked for McGraw. He signed my checks. I was now no more a crusader than he. So I guess I grew up too. I wasn't going back to delivering pizzas. But I also didn't have to be his groupie. Not as I once was. Not anymore. The bloom was off the rose or however that goes. I could assert myself that little bit. When he would offer to take the staff to dinner or when he invited us to his house for a holiday party, I passed. I came to work each day and clocked out each night. At home, I opened the fridge and had a cold one and another one after that and another one until all I thought about was getting to bed before I nodded out. The next morning I got up and made it to work. I did my job, never called in sick, as much as I sometimes wanted to. I gave McGraw that much and no more.

The wind picks up and the fog swirls until it blocks my view of McGraw. A Muni Metro bus wheezes past disturbing pigeons pecking at trash on the street. I don't know how long I've been staring at McGraw, but I can't stand here all morning, although with this headache I really don't feel like talking to him. I cross Leavenworth, wade through homeless people already gathering outside Fresh Start.

We don't open until nine, you all know that, I remind them, as the loose line swings to one side so I can pass through and unlock the security gate.

Tom Murray, Walter shouts.

I turn around. He hands me a cup of coffee with his right hand, holds another steaming cup in his left. He offers me the change. I can't help but smile. I had him all wrong this morning.

Keep it, I tell him. You'll ask me for it later. Now, I got the jump on you.

He gives me a knowing grin, puts the money in his pocket.

I got to talk to you, Tom Murray.

About what?

The clothes closet.

You already did, I say. Wait until we open, Walt.

I open the gate, close it behind me and unlock the door. Inside, light filters through the frayed, closed curtains. Metal folding chairs stand piled against the walls. A clipboard lies at an angle on the front desk. The floor, mopped from the night before, still smells of bleach. Shadows envelop a cubicle used by my benefits advocate. Missing persons fliers tacked to a bulletin board curl at the edges. Conscious of all the eyes on me from outside, I take a deep breath, let the silence sink in.

Another deep breath.

Exhale.

Again.

Listen.

Nothing.

No noise.

I take a final breath and notice one of my homeless volunteers, the Iraq War vet Jay Spencer, standing at the top of the stairs by a desk I gave him, his station to answer the phone. He has a wide face, stocky build. His short red hair points up from his scalp with the precision of shorn grass.

Morning, Tom, Jay shouts.

Hey, Jay, I say.

Jay has post-traumatic stress disorder. He used to come in every morning, sit in the reception area, and refuse to speak. How do you get someone to talk? I asked myself. I had never taken a counseling course. I decided I just had to force him. So I made him our volunteer receptionist.

For two days, the phone rang and rang while Jay sat beside it as if he didn't hear it.

Jay! I yelled. Answer the phone!

He looked at me. He turned toward the phone as if he had just noticed it. He reached for the receiver. In a barely audible voice thick as syrup he said, Fresh Start. May I help you? He listened for a moment and then told me the caller was from Goodwill. They were asking for me. They had some clothes they could give us. I thanked Jay and took the call. In a world of reduced expectations, Jay meets my definition of success.

Mr. McGraw's in your office.

I go up the stairs and stop at Jay's desk.

I see that, thanks. He let you in?

Yes, sir, Jay says.

I look through the window of my office door and watch

McGraw fussing with papers on my desk. It looks like he's organized them into piles beside a stack of crisp manila folders. That's what he does with his desk when he's nervous. Organizes papers. Tidies up. Every year, when the city threatens to reduce our funding or when he's behind on grant applications or when he has appointments with potential donors, McGraw reorganizes his files like it's priority number one.

I set my coffee down and stand outside my office. McGraw looks up.

Hey, Tom, he says. He gets from behind my desk and opens the door a little too fast so that he stumbles when he steps back.

You don't have to knock. Your office.

He laughs a little too loud. I drag my fingertips over the pile of files.

I can actually see my desk.

You can arrange it any way you like, he said, but I find putting folders with budget stuff and other financial things in one of the top drawers of your cabinet and files with program information below them works best for me.

Thanks.

Staff folders go behind the files with the flow charts and our five-year plan.

Got it.

You really should be better organized. There're grants coming up that we need to apply for soon.

Get me the application and I'll fill it out, whatever you need.

You don't run an independent ship. Fresh Start is part of New Horizons.

Never said it wasn't.

You're accountable. You need to be a team player.

I am.

Here's an opportunity to show me.

He gives another forced laugh, picks at his left thumbnail, and rubs his nose. I'm about to offer him a Kleenex when he pulls a file and hands it to me: Okri, Bobby. Bobby is one of my four floor supervisors.

We have to change the status of this guy, Okri.

Why? I ask.

He takes Bobby's folder, opens it, and removes the two pages inside and tears them in half and then tears them again.

Make a new file for Okri. List him as a homeless volunteer.

He's staff.

He's dead, Tom.

McGraw drops the sheets in the trash. One flutters to the side and I pick it up. I look at it and then let it fall from my hand into the trash.

Dead?

Dead.

What happened?

McGraw rubs his face and sighs.

OD'd. Someone found him in his room after the fire alarm went off. Apparently when he passed out he had a cigarette going and it lit up the curtains in his room. Not bad, but the fire department was called and evacuated the building. TV showed up. He had his staff badge in his wallet. Police called me.

I don't know what to say. I'd known Bobby since I started working for McGraw. He was a big old dude in a cowboy hat, jeans, and a T-shirt—the top of which was covered by a thick gray beard. He came in every morning for coffee and called me Kid. Hey, Kid, you're taking this job too serious. Smile! And I would. He had been a Navy cook and volunteered in the kitchen. He made good casseroles out of government-issue cheese, canned pork, and rice. Heavy but edible. Maybe not so much pepper next time, he'd say. A little more cream of mushroom soup. Like he was Julia Child. A personable guy, Bobby. Always used our bathrooms to clean himself with a washcloth after spending a night in Golden Gate Park. He would stink of sweat and camp-fires but never of booze. When he came out of the bathroom, he rolled his sleeves down. He'd shot heroin and speed when he was younger, and his track marks embarrassed him.

He listened well. Whenever we had somebody who had burned all their bridges with alcohol programs, who had been eighty-sixed from all the shelters and just wanted to start a bar fight in the middle of the drop-in, I'd send for Bobby. He'd chill the guy right out until they had it together enough to leave the building without busting any heads.

My contract requires me to hire the homeless, the idea being that people with problems can help other people with problems. I select my staff from the few among them who get clean, or short of that, ones like Bobby, who keep it together despite their vices. If nothing else, they know their world. One time on my way to a meeting, I saw a shelter client holding a knife to a vol-unteer's throat. Bobby was standing beside the guy calm as calm can be. I paused, considered the knife. Serrated edge. Maybe a Gerber, I didn't know. The volunteer's eyes were so wide I half expected to see planets orbiting around them. He had his hands raised above his head and sweat was waxing his face to a shine. He could not have sat more still if he'd tried.

What's going on? I asked.

Nothing, Bobby said, I got this.

A late afternoon mood swing?

Something like that, yeah, he said.

You got this covered?

Yeah. Bobby said.

Do I know you? I asked the guy with the knife.

He looked at me, eyebrows puckered in thought.

I don't think so.

We're good here, Bobby said.

OK, I said and left for my meeting.

When I returned an hour later, Bobby was working the front desk. He told me the guy with knife had wanted a bus token and got pissed off when the volunteer didn't have one. So he threatened to slit the volunteer's throat. Bobby chilled the dude and the volunteer quit. I wonder why, I said, and we both laughed. Bobby handled it, no one died, all good. Plenty more volunteers where that one came from. Another example of a positive outcome in a world of reduced expectations.

I don't know how Bobby chilled people, but it's a skill I appreciate more than I can say. He was someone I could depend on. So when I had a staff opening, I hired him. With his first paycheck he rented a room in the Higgins Hotel about a block away. I offered to put him in The Bridge but he said he didn't want a program with staff looking at him cross-eyed, wondering if he was using. A place to lay his head free of any hassle. I'd see him come in to work with his hair wet and slicked to one side from a shower and I used to tease him about how he no longer washed in our bathroom. You're costing me a hygiene stat, I told him. But I gave you a housing one, he said.

This is the holiday season, Tom, McGraw says. I shouldn't have to tell you that Christmas is the time of year when we do our biggest fundraising. It doesn't look good when you're trying to raise money and one of your staff ODs and starts a fire. You think the commissioners won't ask me about this?

He starts pacing. He picks at his fingers some more, bites his upper lip. I know what he's thinking: The commissioners will want answers. They wouldn't care about our contract. Why had we hired an imperfect homeless guy? They'd needle McGraw and they'd enjoy needling him. The press would likely pick up on it:

A staff member of Fresh Start, a program of New Horizons, is among the dead. Drugs are suspected.

We need to take Bobby off the staff list, McGraw says.

The city gets the staff list every month with my services report. They have his name already.

Then tell us what to do, Tom. This isn't just my problem.

I drag a hand over my head, my heart thumping. Jesus, whatever happens McGraw's going to make it out to be my fault. I really wish I hadn't cut Mary off last night. I don't know what I want from her, but I sure feel alone right now. Like a little kid lost in a mall, that kind of alone. I try to think, break it down. How close, really, do the people at DSS review the information I send them? They get the same stack of forms from all the other agencies. If they read every piece of paper they'd never go home. So they probably don't. Most likely. Therefore, we can fudge.

If anyone asks, we can say we paid Bobby when he filled in for somebody out sick. He worked as a sub. He wasn't staff. Not like regular staff.

McGraw stops pacing. He turns his head toward me, a smile creeping across his face.

We always give volunteers a chance by hiring them as subs, he says.

They make mistakes.

We were giving Bobby a chance just like our other volunteers. Look at all the people we've helped.

We have that in the stats? McGraw asks. The numbers of people we helped get into drug programs and helped get jobs.

Of course, I say. I turn that in too, every month.

McGraw stares at me hard. After a moment, he throws his head back and laughs and we high five and I start laughing too. We're like addicts ourselves, racing from one crisis to the next, thrilled when we avert disaster. I have no respect for the guy, but I'm hooked. Sorry, Bobby. I really am. I don't want to think about him now. I will later when I'm home and drinking a beer. He might appreciate that.

I notice McGraw looking at me again. No smile. I'd never known that a second ago he was all kinds of relieved. Like he just puts the brakes on as if something unseen had snapped its fingers. He keeps staring at me for what feels like a long time.

There's something else, he says finally. One of your staff, Harrison, I think?

Yeah. Frank Harrison. I fired him. What about him?

He came to my office yesterday. He says you drink on the job.

Bullshit.

That's what he said.

And what did you say?

Do you drink at work, Tom?

I hold his stare.

You approved the termination.

This is not about his termination. It doesn't look good when you got a staff member overdosing and starting fires and his program director is accused of drinking at work by a terminated employee.

McGraw drums his fingers on my desk.

He's saying it because he was terminated.

I don't know if the commissioners will see it that way.

If I told you Frank had said this about you, you'd laugh in my face.

He's not saying it about me.

I try to stay calm. Fog pebbles the window with droplets. Car horns just below me on Leavenworth blare but sound far off. The pain in my temples is on overdrive. I hear the pounding in my head.

Check my evals, I say slowly to keep my voice from shaking. With anger, fear, both. You wrote them. Bumped my pay up after each one. I don't remember you mentioning I had a drinking problem.

No one was saying anything about you then.

I'm out of words and feel exhausted. My heart beats in panic. I want to sit. I keep standing.

It doesn't have to be a termination, Tom. I can call it a layoff. Blame it on a funding cut. I'll give you references.

All because of a fired employee's accusation?

I can offer you severance. A good package.

Me and Bobby, I say.

It's not like that.

What's it like?

I told you. Right or wrong it doesn't look good, Tom.

I look out my window at the YMCA across the street. I see young women stretching in an aerobics class. Young, long brown hair, tight black leggings. Leaning to the left and then to the right, arms thrust upward. I see a woman with a boombox. She sets it down and within seconds the whole room erupts, the women shaking to tunes I can't hear. The bright room wrapped in gold light. I feel their joy. Even Jay watches them.

I can't stop Frank from lying about me because he's pissed off I fired him.

Do you drink at work? McGraw asks again.

I work at work.

I hear something clatter in the hall and McGraw and I look out the door. Jay is leaning over his desk. The phone lies on the floor, two lines blinking. Jay sits back, folds his arms, and starts to laugh.

You don't run an independent ship, Tom, McGraw says, watching Jay. You just watch yourself and watch who you hire. And you can clear more of your ranks today starting with Jay.

Jay?

Yeah. He really should be on disability.

We're working on it.

Have him mop floors if you want but take him off the reception desk. You need someone normal answering your phones.

McGraw drags a finger over a cabinet and looks at it for dust. He notices a piece of paper with some notes on it from last week's staff meeting and hands it to me.

You should file this.

I take it, drop it in a trash bin without a glance. McGraw shakes his head as if I'm beyond hope. Maybe I am. He goes out without another word and doesn't close the door behind him. Pausing at Jay's desk, he picks up the phone. Jay stops laughing and thanks him. McGraw checks for a dial tone. Then he walks down the stairs.

I look at the wall clock. Almost nine. I've got a few minutes to talk to Jay. Won't take long. Maybe I'll make mopping the floors sound like the job of the century. Maybe I'll put him back on the phone when things settle down and McGraw won't notice. Maybe Jay won't care. Him and Bobby. My morning.

I rub my temples. I'm sweating. I'm definitely going to have a beer at lunch. Screw Frank. Maybe he did smell beer on my breath one day, I don't care. So much for those grilled cheese sandwiches. Bottom line, I'm here and he's not. I still wish Mary was with me, meeting me for lunch or something. If I call her, I'll have to apologize for blowing her off last night and I'll feel worse. If she says she can see me after work I'll get home and just cancel on her again, I know it. I'll open the fridge for a beer, just one, and then it will be two and three and that'll be it, I won't see her. But God it'd be nice to be with her right now. Someone. Just to be told everything will be all right. It's so quiet. So nice and quiet. My favorite part of the day is right before we open, that and when I get home and pop open my first Bud and relax.

I let out a long breath, massage my temples again, and get up and open the door.

Jay, I got to talk to you but first I need you to go out and get me another coffee and some Advil, OK? You know what? Screw the coffee. Just the Advil. Would you do that for me please?

Walter

Matt lights a cigarette, asks me in a voice a little thick from drinking, Why do you think we come here?

This, I say and raise my beer.

He laughs, slaps my shoulder, and gets quiet. After a moment, he says, Have you heard about my condition?

I turn to him. John and Dennis, two regulars seated on the other side of Matt, expectantly face him too. The noise of a pool game drifts out from the other room.

No, I say sipping my beer. No, I haven't heard about your condition.

I see Matt, John, and Dennis in the Comeback Club when I get my general assistance check and can pay bar prices. They come here every day, I think. I don't have that kind of cash. I'll be back at Fred's buying bottles of T-bird in a few days. He lets me run a tab. Every month I pay him off cutting into the scratch I can spare to drink at the Comeback.

My condition is that I've got lymphoma, Matt says. Cancer.

John's eyebrows leap up and Dennis jerks back like he's been slapped. Matt bites his lower lip and shakes his head, a hangdog look crosses his face. He stares into his beer. I don't know what to say. He's a nice guy, a good guy. I feel for him, I surely do, but I don't know him well enough to feel anything in my gut. It doesn't matter to me if I ever see him again. I don't even know his last name. I've been coming to the Comeback long enough to become familiar with some of the regulars like Matt and John and Dennis, but we're not friends. Friends in the sense that we'd ever do something together other than drink here. I come to the Comeback not to talk as much as to get off the bricks and among people.

I'm sorry, I say.

Sorry to hear that, Matt, Dennis says.

What happened? John says.

Matt doesn't answer. The bartender, Gail, acts like she hasn't heard a thing. She turns the thermostat up and begins washing glasses. Warm air washes out of the ceiling vent rocking a hanging basket with dead flowers. I take off my sweatshirt. I feel like I'm going to wilt, but I'm not about to complain. One night when a guy ragged about his drink being weak, Gail pulled down her jeans and exposed her ass, one word on each cheek: KISS THIS.

Well, I went in for a physical a couple of days back just because I hadn't had a physical in a long time, Matt says. Getting near fifty, that sort of thing. Then boom!

Just like that, huh? Dennis says.

Just like that. Boom! The doctor ran some tests and wouldn't you know it, I got cancer. Was feeling fine, man. Really. Still do. Shit.

Matt's a big guy, broad shoulders, arms thick as tree trunks. He works construction. Starts at five o'clock in the morning, clocks out midafternoon, and stops by the Comeback for a beer and then some. He's usually half lit by the time I get here. Sometimes, I am too. He asked me what I do. Handyman, I told him. I got a sign, I'll work for food, I tell him. He laughed, thinks I'm joking.

I stay in a financial district alley behind an Italian restaurant. The Transamerica building pokes into the sky not too far away. It would be a trip, I think, to work there as a window washer. On Tuesday mornings, when garbagemen empty the dumpster, I move my stuff to another alley behind another dumpster behind another restaurant, this one Greek. When it's time to empty that dumpster, I go back to the Italian restaurant alley. At night, I tie one end of a tarp to the dumpster handles and weigh the other end with a cinderblock, making a kind of lean-to. Every three hours the restaurant tosses out food. Something about if it sits around that long it's no good. A few of the kitchen staff drop the food into the dumpster instead of giving it to me, but most of them put it in takeout boxes and set it on the pavement, bending over real slow, keeping just far enough away from me like they're feeding a stray dog that'll bolt if they make a sudden move. There's only so much I can eat. Sometimes I keep a box for the morning. What I can't use I put in the dumpster. I clean up so the restaurant crew keeps giving me food. Scratch my back, scratch yours sort of deal. Every so often I want to talk, tell them I was a manager at a Lowes in Oakland. Tell them how one job can lead to another. It did me. These young kids at the restaurants, it's easy for them to get fed up and quit. I want to tell them to hang in there. I had a few jobs before I landed at Lowes, mostly janitorial, but they gave me the experience I needed. It's hard, though, to talk to people who are afraid you might bite them. I wasn't always like this.

Boom, Matt says again. The fucking ax just falls. Whether you're ready or not, here it comes, off with your head.

I look at him expecting to see something wrong. Like, I don't know, blotches on his skin maybe. Something, but I don't see even a pimple. He looks like he did the last time I saw him. Still built like a brick shithouse, his hands balled loosely into fists the size of boxing gloves. But I guess his hands are no match for what he's dealing with now.

Why do you think we come here?

This, I say again, raising my glass.

Matt laughs, smacks me on the shoulder, and I wobble on my stool, slopping beer on the floor. Kind of pisses me off. I don't have the money to waste beer like that. I mean, coming here, this is a treat for me. Matt continues laughing, laugh lines etching out from around those sad, bloodshot eyes of his.

I'll get Matt his next one, Dennis says.

He shakes an empty Budweiser bottle, and Gail reaches below the bar and gets him another one, dripping ice. Dennis got a DWI a few weeks back, third one I think, driver's license suspended for good this time. I told him he's going to end up like me. But he doesn't know I'm homeless and I'm not about to tell him. We're all equals here. Me, letting him know I'm homeless, would change that. I'm a guy in a bar with other guys in a bar. Kind of nice to be seen that way.

Dennis gets around now on a two-speed bicycle and carries newspaper clippings of the September 11th terrorist attacks that he reads obsessively. He can't get over how guys armed only with box cutters took over three planes. Had he been on board . . . His voice drifts and the rest of us don't pay attention. Dennis couldn't bust a grape.

Well, after tonight no more beer and cigarettes, Matt says, exhaling a plume of smoke that lingers in the air, then stretches into thin gray fingers sucked up by a ceiling fan. I'm getting treatment. But I ain't going to do that chemo thing.

What're you going to do instead? I ask.

I got some buddies in LA. There're things you can do with oxygen, herbal remedies. Natural things. I'm leaving for there tomorrow. See what they can do for me. If I go out, it won't be under no chemo. No way.

There ain't nothing you can do about it, except pray, John says.

Thanks man, Matt says and squeezes the back of John's neck.

John shrugs him off and asks Gail for a shot of Jack and a beer. You'll be all right, John tells Matt.

I first met John here one night when he asked me if I knew who had won the previous night's Chiefs game. I told him I didn't follow football. I was reading a copy of the San Francisco Chronicle someone had left on the bar and handed him the sports page. How about basketball? he said. I shook my head. I don't follow that either. I went back to reading the paper. He flicked a finger in my face.

Hey! I said.

I'm talking to you. Don't you have a TV?

No, actually, I don't

Jesus, what kind of person doesn't have a TV?

Until recently, John had been seeing the daytime bartender, Bonnie. He would stop by at noon during her shift and have lunch with her. When he got off work, he came back and waited until she punched out. Then they would go to his place for pizza and Netflix. Bonnie had nothing better going on. The way Gail tells it, Bonnie chewed John up and spit him out in no time flat and took up with another guy, a real estate agent. John installs kitchen cabinets, drives a pickup. Real Estate Man doesn't work with his hands. He takes Bonnie to restaurants. I mean downtown restaurants. He takes her to the theater and they've enrolled in a tango dance class together. John doesn't have it in him to offer Bonnie the two-step.

Why do you come here? Matt asks John.

Because, John says and raises his glass.

Fair enough, Matt says.

He blows at the foam on his beer.

We all die sometime. I just wasn't expecting to now, he says.

You're not dead yet, Matt, I say.

I suppose this'd kill me as well.

35

Don't I know it, I say.

We all get our ticket punched, don't we?

I couldn't argue with that. Matt stands and walks stiff legged to a popcorn machine.

I'll pray for him, Gail says. She smells of the soap she uses to wash the glasses. During the day, she's a cashier at the Best Buy in Oakland. Just the other week, she told me, a gal who had worked there five years was laid off.

I sip my beer, watch her turn the lights down, and stare at myself in the mirror behind the bar. I see only the dim, circular outline of my head, my face obscured by the shadows curtaining the mirror. I should get back to my alley, but it's nice here. I live light. When I first hit the streets, I had a shopping cart, but it got so I was acting like I still had a home. I collected stuff, like everybody does, unnecessary stuff, clothes and blankets—more than I could possibly use. And I had to pack it up every time I left my camp so no one would steal it. The cart became a weight like so much else in life. So I walked away from it as I did my apartment when I thought all I had to do was move, stop drinking, get right, and I'd be OK and would get everything back I'd lost, but by then all the helium had leaked out of the balloon, so to speak, and there was no renewal on the horizon. I've been in detox programs. Moving to escape your problems is what you call a geographic. At least that's what alcohol counselors have told me. I don't know why everything has to have a name. It's kind of a judgment. You did a geographic, like that's bad. Man, I only wanted to get away, call it what you want. These days, I spend a few nights in shelters when it gets cold, but most don't let you in if you smell of alcohol so I go back to my alley. I guess that's kind of doing a geographic too. This stuff gets in your head. I wish I could just stay here at the Comeback.

Do you think Matt'll make it? John asks, leaning over to me.

I look at him over by the popcorn machine. At the patchy beard on his face and at the faded blue work shirt cut off at the sleeves and at the loose threads stuck to his arm. I can't see Bonnie ever having dreamed long-buried dreams with John as I presume she does now with Real Estate Man. I see Real Estate Man put his hands on her waist. He holds her on the dance floor turning her in ever-widening circles, making those dreams seem possible.

I don't know if he will or not, John, I say.

I don't either, Dennis says.

Matt sits back down holding a bowlful of popcorn.

Want some popcorn?

No, thanks.

You got a wife? Matt asks me.

Nope, I tell him.

I don't either. I got a girlfriend. She's not talking to me. Last night, we got into it over her daughter. She's like ten. The three of us were having dinner together and all of a sudden her daughter shoves her plate aside and says she hates chicken. Last week, chicken was fine. Same dinner, no complaints. Tonight chicken, and rice and peas, and a salad were cause for a tantrum. And what does my girlfriend do? She gets up from the table and goes out and buys her daughter Taco Bell. I thought that was crazy, so we got into it. On and on until we ran out of words, ran out of breath. I'm leaving her. I know it. I just don't know when. I need something that will give me a reason to say, I'm done. We're through. Taco Bell didn't provide that. I mean I can't say, my gal got her daughter a bacon ranch tortada and that was it. I had it. I walked. People would laugh. What I'm saying is, when I leave her it has to count for something.

He picks at the popcorn but doesn't eat it. I look out a window. Ellis Street is pitch black. How'd it get so late? A bus stop stands empty. Nothing moves.

I got to go, I say.

And do what?

He had me there. Go to my camp. Drink some more there. I should have a bottle of T-bird stashed. We all have our schedules. More like routines, I guess. The restaurant I stay behind got robbed twice in the past week. Last night, when I got back I saw that the owner was installing bars over the windows. He doesn't have a problem with me sleeping in the alley so I helped him and he gave me a few bucks. I told him he didn't have to, but he insisted, Here, take it. I didn't do much but hold the bars while he drilled holes and screwed them in. When we finished he went his way and I went mine. I liked helping him, showing him I could be useful. Maybe I'll do more of that with him, I don't know. No point to go thinking that far ahead.

Good luck, I tell Matt. I hope to see you again.

I hope to see you again too.

That strikes me as funny and I laugh and so does he. We're almost hysterical. One of those moments when you forget where you are and you laugh for no good reason.

I get up, slip on my coat. Matt stands too. I reach to shake his hand, and he wraps me in a back-breaking bear hug burying my face in his T-shirt, and I'm swamped by the rankness of cigarette smoke and sweat.

Why do we come here, man?

I try to pull away but he holds me. I feel his heart race, can't talk, and shake my head.

Because we're scared, Matt says. I think it's because we're scared.

Katie

I get off at eleven, come home, and usually watch some YouTube on my phone and put off sleep and the nightmares, but tonight I take a shower because I had to help a man who pissed himself, and even though I had put on plastic gloves and washed my hands afterward, I still felt kind of gross.

The shower must've relaxed me because I nod off and have a drinking dream. I see the guy who pissed himself raise a bottle, swallow, and then pass it to me. Just as I tip it to my mouth, I feel Stacey beside me. I'm not saying a word, she says. She takes the bottle from me and polishes it off. I'm in no position to comment, she says and wipes her mouth. I wake up in the dark. What are you doing? I say to her fading image. I don't move. The dark consumes her absence. I lie on my bed until I remember I'm in my room. I had a dream about Stacey. Stacey. Shit. She's my AA sponsor. Was. Last month she started drinking again.

I'm an intake worker for the twenty-four-hour alcohol detox program at Fresh Start. I come in for the swing shift. This afternoon, I clock in just as one of our regulars, Walter Johns, struts through the door slick as he can be.

Look at you, my supervisor Rosemary says.

We have a fat folder on Walter but today you'd never know it. He's wearing a brown corduroy jacket, white shirt and brown tie, and blue jeans. Lines river his tanned face and a ceiling fan disturbs his slicked-back hair, unraveling strands against his forehead that he keeps batting from his eyes. His clothes are typical thrift store stuff but clean and pressed; they fit him well. If I didn't know him, I'd assume he was a normal guy.

Look at you, old 357, Rosemary says again, and she gives this deep ha, ha belly laugh that creases her cheeks with a smile and makes me smile too. Three fifty-seven is Walter's file number. Rosemary avoids calling clients by their name to keep her distance, so when they start drinking again it doesn't bother her. I think it still does. It does me. You can't help but get to know people if you see them every day but sometimes you just have to pretend it doesn't bother you, and I guess that's how Rosemary pretends.

That's Mr. 357 to you, Walter tells Rosemary and she falls into that laugh again.

Walter, where've you been? I ask him.

Salvation Army's recovery center.

He raises two fingers.

Two months.

If I wasn't as old as your mother I'd give you a second look, Rosemary says, and I swear Walter blushes.

Katie, Walter goes, give me a cigarette.

Give me? They teach you no manners at Sally's? They pay you?

Like prison. A dollar an hour.

For two months. How many hours in two months, Walter?

C'mon, Katie.

I pull my purse from a file cabinet and give him a smoke. Rosemary asks him his plans. He shrugs.

You need a plan, Rosemary scolds. Have you signed up for a halfway house?

I'll be all right, Walter says.

At that moment I know he plans to start drinking again and Rosemary knows it too. He has a plan; the plan is to drink. Don't assume, Stacey would tell me, but I know.

Walter wanders around some tables in the waiting room where a handful of guys slouch in chairs trying not to pass out before we do their intakes. He pauses, greets people he knows. Almost like a guy picking up a day labor crew. He shows them his Salvation Army name badge. They know he has money. He walks toward the door. They wobble to their feet and follow him.

And off they go. Rosemary mutters, staring after them.

About fifteen minutes before I clock out, Walter weaves through the door stumbling forward like someone is pulling him by the nose. Somehow he lost his shoes and his bare feet are bloody. He's pissed himself. He leans against a drinking fountain, picks a broken cigarette from an ashtray, and holds it uncertainly. Sinking to the floor, he shouts for Rosemary and me. A bottle of Thunderbird tilts out of his jacket pocket.

Jesus, you couldn't even last a day, Rosemary snaps.

I go to a cabinet, pull his file—Johns, Walter, No. 357—and drop it on a desk. I pull out a chair and sit. Walter starts crying. Rosemary yells at him to get up. He lurches over to me and collapses in a chair. I search a drawer for a pen.

I want a program, Walter says, slurring.

You just left one.

I want another one.

I write today's date in his file. Previous intakes all say the same thing: Johns says he has been drinking about twenty years. His last drink, he says, was minutes before this intake. Wants a program. No one grows up wishing to be an alcoholic, Stacey would tell me, but no one makes them drink either. They can quit if they choose. Don't take on someone else's sobriety. Concentrate on your own.

Stacey's husband died of a heart attack while he was jogging. He wasn't a drinker, never had a problem with booze. Forty something. Could have happened to anybody. Just like that.

Accept the things you cannot change, but Stacey couldn't. She had been ten years clean and sober when she started drinking again a week after he died. She lives with her daughter, Nancy, now. Nancy told me to stop calling. My mom is no longer available to you, she said.

After I finish Walter's intake, I take him to detox, a large room on the other side of a divider that separates it from the waiting area. Twenty exercise mats with blankets, sheets cover the tile floor. Four small tables form a horseshoe around a kitchenette. Chicken noodle soup is warming on a hot plate beside a plate of peanut butter and jelly sandwiches. A door behind the kitchenette leads into a woman's dorm.

Mat number ten, Walter, I say. You want something to eat?

He shakes his head, dive bombs onto his mat, and passes out.

I punch out and walk home. I rent a room at The Bridge, a two-year transitional housing hotel for recovering alcoholics and addicts on Ellis, north of Market Street in the Tenderloin. I've got another twelve months before I'll have to move out. I try not to think about that although I should, I know. Have a plan. I take an elevator to my third-floor room and throw my purse on my bed and open my window. Fog rolls in off San Francisco Bay. I have a K-cup coffee machine and knee-high refrigerator that just fits beneath my sink. I make a ham sandwich on my bed and brush the crumbs to the floor. When I'm done eating, I brush my teeth, change into pj's, shut off the lights, and stretch out. The neon vacancy sign of a hotel across the street blinks on and off, striping my blanket with blue and red lights.

Down the hall, this chick and her boyfriend, both of them recovering crackheads, are going at it screaming at each other. The building manager, Larry, will be humping it to our floor in a minute to see what all's going on. He's been sober five years, lives on the first floor, and assumes we're all chipping. He frisks visitors to see if they're carrying booze. Residents complain, but Larry turns it around on them. If your friend's clean what's the problem with a pat down? He'll check on these two idiots and then he'll knock on all our doors to see what the rest of us are up to.

Kicking out of bed, I turn on my night table lamp and get a smoke. Might as well wait for Larry. My shadow spreads like a stain against the wall as I stand and make coffee. I like it strong to get a little speed rush. Won't last but it feels good, and there's not a goddamn thing Larry can do about it. Stinkin' thinkin', Stacey would say, but she's in no place to judge.

I hear the elevator doors open followed by the heavy steps of Larry's gunslinger strut and then I hear him knocking on the couple's door. They shut up in an instant like something switched off. I sit on my bed and slouch against the wall, listening to the coffee drip. After a moment, I hear Larry knock on another door as he begins working his way down the hall. The crackheads must've been clean, because he didn't spend any kind of time with them. When he knocks on my door I don't answer. I feel guilty about my anticipated coffee buzz. I've done nothing, the coffee isn't even ready yet. Still, I'm afraid to answer.

The next afternoon I punch in at work and look at a clipboard to see how many people we have in detox. Just five intakes. Walter's still here. Rosemary tells me a social worker is trying to get him into a long-term detox but he's been through so many programs no one wants him. Even Sally's won't take him back. He's slouched at a table with a bowl of soup. Circles beneath his eyes like the mouths of caves. He holds a spoon poised over the bowl. His hand shakes and the soup slops onto the table. A woman sitting across from him rests her chin in her hands and stares at a wall. I don't see her name on the clipboard. Rosemary tells me she's not here for detox. She just completed an alcohol program at San Francisco General Hospital and is waiting for a halfway house. None of the women's shelters have any spare beds and she has no place to stay. General sent her to us. She spent the morning in the waiting area. Rosemary sent her over to detox to get something to eat.

What's her name?

I didn't ask, Rosemary says.

Why?

She's not in detox.

I sit at a desk and begin reading a National Geographic someone left. Every half hour I get up and check on anyone asleep in detox to make sure they're still breathing. The woman drums her fingers against the table. A stuffed plastic bag filled with clothes sags against her feet.

There's coffee by the soup, I tell her.

I'm OK, she goes. Thanks.

She gives a weak smile. I smile back.

You can use the showers in the women's dorm if you want.

OK.

I go back to my desk and pick up the National Geographic again. The woman nods off, her chin bouncing against her chest. Her head lolls to one side and eyes snap open. I can see the momentary confusion in her face. Folding her arms, she rests a cheek against her hands and closes her eyes.

Why don't we give her a bed? I ask Rosemary.

Because she's not in detox.

She's sitting in detox.

But she's not in detox.

Rosemary has been clean and sober for twenty-odd years and is big on rules. She believes if you bend them at work you'll bend them in your life, and that will lead to drinking.

Let's give her a blanket at least, I say.

Rosemary scowls but doesn't object. I go to the laundry room, take a blanket, and fold it around the woman. She wakes up and I tell her it's OK, just a blanket. She pulls it around her. I pat her back and return to my desk.

Tonight, I have another drinking dream. I'm in the Mission with a bottle of Thunderbird at the Sixteenth Street Muni station. Two police officers haul me to my feet and throw me in the back of a paddy wagon. We're dropping you off at Fresh Start, one of them says. I beg them not to. I work there, I say, I'll lose my job. One of the officers turns to me. It's Stacey. You didn't follow your program, she says. You used your husband as an excuse to drink, I tell her. I was sober for ten years. You barely lasted twelve months. And she shoves me out of the van at Fresh Start just as I wake up.

In the afternoon, I bring my copy of the Big Book with me to work. I clock in and check the clipboard. Eight clients. Walter has been kept over again. He sits across from the woman. They're both smoking. I presume the overnight shift let her stay. I walk through detox, do my head count, and then stop at their table. Her hair hangs limply around her face and she's wearing the same clothes as she did yesterday.

You stayed last night? I ask her.

And all day today, she says.

She made the coffee this morning, Walter says.

He looks better. His hands don't shake.

I wanted to keep busy, she says.

You should clean up, I tell her. Change your clothes. You'll feel better

I'm all right.

No, you're not, I tell her. When we're on the street we don't take care of ourselves. You're not on the street.

What would you call it? she says.

You're in recovery. You're waiting on a halfway house. Where are you on the waiting list?

One person ahead of me. Maybe I'll get in tomorrow or the next day. What do you think?

I offer her the Big Book.

Expectations are premeditated resentments, I say, quoting from it. Focus on the good things happening now. Today you're not drinking.

Yeah, I know, she says, a note of annoyance in her voice. She picks up the Big Book but doesn't open it. It'll help while you wait. C'mon.

I'm tired of waiting. I just want someone to tell me what to do. I get bored waiting.

A pitying look crosses Walter's face. He reaches over and pats her hands.

Hang in there, right? she says. A day at a time?

Sometimes it's a minute at a time, I tell her. C'mon.

I pick up her bag of clothes and walk her to the women's dorm and point to a closet inside the bathroom where we keep towels, soap, and shampoo. I point to a shower.

Wash up and bring your dirty clothes out and we'll wash them, I say.

I remember the last time I was in detox. Rosemary was doing a head count. I had come in the night before and was on a mat. She stood above me with a clipboard and put a check mark by my bed number. Do you want a program? she asked. I did, I told her. OK, she said, and went to the next person. I got referred to a five-day detox.

The morning of my fourth day, a counselor drove me to a forty-five-day inpatient program in Redwood City. When I finished, I got into Oliver House, a halfway house south of Market. Stacey ran AA meetings there once a week. She asked me if I had a sponsor. I didn't. I'll be your sponsor, she said. I didn't even ask her. Didn't have to. She just took me on.

Six months later, Larry accepted me into The Bridge. My lease required me to volunteer at Fresh Start ten hours a week until I found a job. I mopped floors and served coffee for about a month when one of the intake workers quit and I got offered his job. PA one, Rosemary called me. Program assistant, level one. I was seven months sober before she began calling me Katie.

The woman walks out of the female dorm. She's put on a clean pair of jeans and a pink sweatshirt. Her wet, tangled hair drops to her shoulders, and I realize I forgot to give her a comb. Walter whistles. I give him a look and she smiles. I wave her over and she follows me to the laundry room. I point to a washing machine and she dumps her dirty clothes in it. I add soap, close the lid, turn the dial to warm, and press start. We wait until we hear the sound of water running. She turns to me, follows me out, and rejoins Walter. He looks up at her and grins.

Later in the shift, she and Walter wipe down the tables in the waiting room. He says something and she laughs. Her hair is tied back into a ponytail and she's put on eyeliner. She sees me and smiles and Walter flashes me a grin—and for a moment I have this thought of a brother and sister.

You want some coffee? the woman asks me.

Sure, thanks. Rosemary has you working.

I didn't ask. I just want to keep busy. Tell me what to do.

Work your program.

I had things to do at General. I don't know what else to do here but wait.

Work your steps.

I sound like a textbook. Stacey had a way of talking that would have made it sound fresh. Work your steps rolled out of her mouth like, Good morning, natural and cheerful. I feel weak and worthless, because nothing I say is going to sound as good as it would coming from Stacey. I'm scared, scared to think of her so lost, scared at how fragile we both are, and scared that I can't call her.

I watch our interloper go back to detox and pour coffee into a foam cup. Walter follows her, gives her a packet of sugar and a plastic stir stick. She takes the stick, flicks coffee in his face, laughs at his surprised look, and brings me the cup.

The phone rings and Rosemary takes it. When she gets off, she comes over to my desk. That was the social worker, she says. He can't help Walter. No program will take him. He'll have to leave tomorrow morning. It's almost time to go home. Let the overnight shift tell him. I don't want to take that on, do you?

I shake my head no. I don't think he'll be upset. He definitely won't be surprised. But he'll give that sad look that all us drunks give when for a moment we recognize how bad we've fucked up, and then he'll shake it off and do what we all do and drink again. I don't need that look right now.

The woman and Walter wipe more tables. When they finish she pours two cups of coffee and they sit down. Walter covers his face like she'll zing him again and they both laugh. She's coming out of her shell with him. That's scary too, that it's Walter she's leaning on.

She leafs through my copy of the Big Book, closes it, lights a smoke, and exhales massively into Walter's face. He waves a hand and pretends he's choking, and she opens the Big Book again, closes it, and pushes it toward him, and they start laughing for no reason, the book an island between them.

Tonight, I dream about getting drunk on Ocean Beach. I'm panhandling at a stoplight on the Great Highway. No sign, I just walk from car to car when the light's red and ask the drivers if they can help me out. Most people roll up their windows and stare straight ahead. I'm so cold, I say to the drivers, I'm so cold. I hold onto their door handles and they take off and I tumble to the pavement. An ambulance stops and two paramedics get out and ask if I'm all right. Blood runs down my left side. They clean me up and give me a blanket and tell me to be careful. Have you been drinking? They ask. No, I tell them. The truth now, one of them says in Stacey's voice. I hold the blanket, shaking. You're in no position to talk, I say. I wake up to the sound of my voice shouting at her, curled in a corner of my bed shouting.

When I come into work this afternoon, I check the clipboard and do a head count. I don't see the woman.

Where's the lady waiting for the halfway house? I ask Rosemary.

Gone.

She get in?

No, she says.

What then?

She left.

Left?

With Walter.

I let that sink in for a minute.

The morning shift kicked her out with him?

No, the night shift told him his time was up and this morning when he left she went with him. No one made her. She just walked out with him.

I try to ignore Rosemary's I-told-you-so look.

I guess she got tired of waiting, I say finally.

Tired of waiting, Rosemary repeats, the sarcasm in her voice impossible to miss. She got tired, yeah, got tired of not drinking.

I take the clipboard and do a head count. The woman will come back and this time she'll need detox. She's not a number, not yet, but soon, I know. Soon. Look after your own recovery,

49

Stacey would say. She would be right. There's nothing I can do. It's just me and Rosemary. I never asked the lady her name. That's good, I guess. Rosemary's rubbing off on me. I get it but I hope every so often Stacey thinks of me.

Walter

The phone rings on Oscar's desk just as I ask him for a shower. He raises a hand to stop me from speaking and picks up the receiver.

Fresh Start, he says. Social worker's office. May I help you?

Oscar nods his head to whatever the person on the other end is saying and takes notes. Thank you, he goes and hangs up.

Goddamn it, Walter, he shouts at me. Where's your mask?

I shrug. He points to a sign hanging off the desk: COVID-19 ALERT. WEAR A MASK.

I was going to ask you for one.

Yeah, right.

I come to Fresh Start about once a day at least for a shower and the food bags that Oscar hands out, mostly canned stuff. I got a P-38 if I need it. If you don't have one of those old military can openers or some other kind, and a place to cook, then you eat cold food. Tuna fish cold I can do, other things like canned chili, no. I get a cup of noodles and use the hot water attached to coffee machines in convenience stores to heat it.

A woman comes in and stands behind me. Oscar leans so he can see around me and look at her. He's a fucking dog, man. Oscar turns back to me and points to a jug of hand sanitizer on a stool about a foot from his desk. I spritz it, rub my palms together. The sanitizer turns to goop from my dirty hands. I wipe them on my pants, mixing dead germs with new ones. I show Oscar my smeared palms. He makes a face and extends his right arm, a blue surgical mask dangling off one finger. I put it on.

Thank you, he says.

I need a shower and a food bag, I tell him.

He gives me a plastic sack. I open it. Tuna fish, some crackers, a bottle of water. Good.

Shower?

You want a job, Walter? Oscar asks.

A job?

The person on the phone just now was a guy in North Berkeley. He needs help painting one side of his house.

How big is it?

I don't know. Twelve dollars an hour. You want it?

How long will this take?

Four hours, he thinks. Maybe longer. Why? You busy today, Walter? You have other plans?

I'm just asking.

Up to you.

I don't know. It probably won't take long. Just a room. And it'll be money in my pocket instead of standing on Seventh and Market with my hand out. I need a new sign. I had one: Homeless, anything will help. Thank you. A girl who said she was a student at the Academy of Art University asked to decorate it and made all sorts of swirls with different colored markers. It was the best-looking sign I ever had, got me some money too, for real. Even had a few people take selfies, but cardboard lasts only so long.

What do I say to the guy?

That we referred you to the job, Oscar says. I'll call him back and give him your name. You don't have to say much. This isn't a date.

I don't know.

You been drinking today?

No.

What's that I smell on your breath?

Teeth that need brushing.

He snorts a laugh and tears off a sheet of paper with a name and an address on Eunice Street and tells me to be there by ten. Taking a metal box from a drawer, he gives me a BART pass and ten bucks.

I don't know if he's including lunch, Oscar says.

I take the money.

This enough?

Should be for a sandwich. Of course this is San Francisco, but I think so. Don't drink it up.

I look at him and smile.

I'm serious, Walter.

What about my shower?

You're just going to get dirty on the job. Wash up afterward.

I need a shower.

I don't disagree. I'm just saying.

So I'm doing this?

Are you?

I guess.

I think you should.

This guy in AA?

How'd you know?

You're fooling, right?

He told me he was in recovery and wanted to help a fellow drunk.

A fellow drunk?

My words. Five-minute showers.

I don't want him lecturing me.

Oscar reaches behind his chair and tosses me a white towel.

You don't have to say anything but Thank you.

I go to a table where a guy sits in a chair outside a bathroom. Shower open? I ask him.

Sign in, he tells me, and pushes a clipboard toward me. No one's ahead of you.

May I have a hygiene kit?

I almost said "Can I," but "may" is grammatically correct. My sixth-grade teacher, Miss Fowler, drilled grammar into us. She made us write two-hundred-word essays once a week and blue-lined the hell out of them. I like to think that sets me apart a bit from everyone else.

The volunteer reaches for a box at his feet and hands me a baggie with a razor, soap, a deodorant stick, and a finger-size bottle of shampoo. His hands shake. Fresh Start's twenty-four-hour detox is next door. I don't recognize this guy but I bet he dried out and is waiting for an inpatient program. I don't ask. I've been there. You get tired of people getting into your business. No good comes of it. Someone will go, Where are you on the waiting list? and then you're reminded how long you'll be waiting, and then you think, Screw this, and start drinking.

I walk into the bathroom, pull off my mask, hang my towel on a hook, and take the soap and shampoo out of the baggie. The yellow linoleum floor smells of bleach and shines in the pale light. A bucket of gray dirty water and a mop stand against the shower door. I move them and open the door and turn the knob to hot. I pull my shirt off and drop it on the floor and really catch a dose of my stink. I step out of my pants and the air quality gets even worse. I turn my head so as not to get a dose of my feet when I yank my socks off. Steam rises out of the shower and a shiver goes through me as the water hits the top of my head, and I just stand there, chin against my chest, as the heat waxes over my shoulders. Water bubbles against my arms and I scrub myself three times all over until my skin squeaks beneath my fingers. I rinse myself a final time and shut off the water. Toweling off, I hear the bathroom door crack open.

Time's almost up, the volunteer says.

OK.

I lean against a wall and put on a pair of jeans I picked up at a Goodwill on my way here with a voucher Oscar gave me last week. Got a blue polo shirt and a pair of socks too. I pull the pants up and roll the cuffs because they're a little long. I take my belt from my old pants and tug it through the loops, feeling behind me with my fingers so I don't miss any, and I see myself in a mirror, not fat but sagging around my chest and stomach, every hair gray. A middle-aged man dressing for work, that's me. I slip on the shirt. It falls like a feather against my shoulders. I put toothpaste on the toothbrush and scrub my tongue. I've lost most of my teeth and the few still in my mouth resemble posts from a rotted fence. I rinse my mouth, shave, wipe my face with the towel, and put on my mask. I look at myself again. Not so bad. Can't see my teeth, anyway.

Combing my hair, I think maybe this time I'll stop drinking, for real, and there's this voice in my head that goes, Sure, sure you will, and I hear the sarcasm but it doesn't stop me from thinking maybe, just maybe. I always get this way after a shower, I guess because I feel better and I don't look so ragged. I'm tired from the aches and pains of sleeping outside that pile on with the years. Maybe this is the moment. Maybe. If this job works out, if this guy needs me for other work, if he can keep me busy. It's on him. I'm in his hands. And if he goes all nazi on me with AA, I'm out of there. I don't want to disappoint Oscar, but I'll be gone. I get stressed thinking about it, all these ifs and the things he might say, but I got ten bucks in my pocket to deal with any problems. I don't want to do Oscar like that, but if I can't handle this guy then that's how it'll be. I won't have a choice, not if he pushes my buttons. Try not to worry about him, I tell myself. You're clean. You're back in the game. He'll be cool. Don't trip. I take a deep breath. You can do this. Sure, sure, the voice in my head says.

I pull on the socks. They stick to my feet. I wiggle my toes. The socks cling to the sweaty insides of my sneakers. I take off the shoes, stick the towel in each one, and wipe them out. When I finish I put them on again. That's a little better. Tucking in my shirt, I imagine knocking on the door of the guy in North Berkeley. I'm here about the paint job, I see myself saying. I guess the guy will ask me in. Maybe not. I don't know. My heart ticks up a notch just thinking about it.

Time's up! the volunteer shouts.

I grab my old clothes and hurry out.

Sorry, I say, thanks.

I drop the clothes in a hamper to be washed and recycled for someone else.

I got a job today, I tell the volunteer.

Where at?

North Berkeley.

At least you'll get out of here for a while.

That's what I'm thinking. What about you?

Waiting on a program?

I figured. Which one?

Redwood Center.

It's good.

Been there?

Yeah.

What happened?

What always happens. I started drinking again. Nobody made me. I didn't have to.

I'm like tenth on the waiting list.

Good luck.

Day at a time, right?

That's what they say.

I turn to leave. Passing Oscar's office, I raise my hand goodbye, but he's talking to that gal who was behind me in line. I go out the front doors to the sidewalk. The sun blazes down and I cover my eyes. Cool in the shade, warm in the sun. I like days like this. I feel almost like a normal person. My hands shake a bit, my body talking. Where's that wine? it's asking me. Across the street I see two guys I know, Lonny and Jeffrey. Lonny lost his right leg in a motorcycle accident, or that's what he says. He doesn't have it, I know that much. The accident cost him his job at a garage. He got on disability and started drinking. He always drank, he said, but after the accident he got into it full-time. He has a thick brown beard, and when he listens to people speak he frowns and pouts his lower lip and makes me think of a clam all bristly with that beard. I can't talk to him without laughing. He dried out one time and would have been accepted into a program except for his leg. He had to show he could get out of a room, hop through a hall, and down a flight of stairs in sixty seconds in case of a fire. He hopped like a mofo, but he always fell, even when he used crutches. Nerves, he said. Everybody watching him. The program wouldn't take him and he started drinking again.

If they'd've given me a few seconds more . . . he said. Katie, one of the detox counselors, told him to apply to other programs, but Lonny decided that getting drunk in a doorway was less humiliating.

Lonny raises a hand, and I see he's got a bottle. I wave back but keep walking. If I go over to him I'll start drinking. Then the three of us will blow my ten bucks, and then Oscar will tell me how I burned a resource and ruined it for all the other people this North Berkeley guy could have helped. I cut up Sixth Street and turn on Market toward the Embarcadero to catch a BART train. I don't have to walk, I could catch a bus, but I want to walk. In my clean clothes, strolling to work like everyone else. Nobody knows who I am. They think I'm one of them. I laugh. Shadows retreat, shrink up buildings, slide back on the rooftops. Sweat begins to pool under my arms. I feel a little jittery but good, I'm good. I'll get past the shakes. Sometimes I stay sober for two or three days. I'll have this bloated feeling and I can't drink. Or I just don't feel well. The few hours of the first day sober are hard, not impossible, but hard. On warm days like this they're easier. On cloudy days when the air gives me chills, then it's impossible, and I drink and I won't care how bad I'll feel later, or how down I'll be on myself.

I jog down the steps of the Embarcadero Station, flash my BART pass, and shuffle behind a man pushing through the turnstile to the platform where a train waits, doors open. I have about an hour to spare, more than enough time to get to the job.

I'm going to work, I say to the guy ahead of me.

Another day, another two cents, he says, glancing at me over a shoulder.

The train jerks forward just as I get on and I reach for a pole to keep from falling. An older woman watches me stumble and I smile and then I feel embarrassed for showing her my bad teeth. I lift a hand to hide my mouth, but I feel my mask and realize she can't see my teeth.

That was close, I say, and she smiles back and we both shake our heads as if to say, Isn't this something? The train starting before I can sit down. She adjusts her mask, digs into her purse for a pair of glasses, and starts reading a copy of *The New Yorker*. A subscription card falls out and I pick it up.

Thank you, she says.

I smile again and sit down across from her.

I'm painting a house today, I say. I work at Lowes.

Oh, she replies, looking over the top of her glasses. A good day for it. Weather, I mean. I didn't know Lowes sent people out to do house work.

I shrug.

A house in North Berkeley, I say.

Oh, she goes again. That's where I live. Do you do gutters?

I do, I say. Since I was a kid. Used to clean my mom's gutters.

Well, mine need to be done, the lady goes. Do you have a card?

I don't.

She takes out her cell phone.

What's the Lowes number?

I hesitate for a minute and then make up a number. If she calls, she'll think she misheard me or put it in her phone wrong. At least that's what I hope. I want her to believe I work.

I can do your gutters, I tell her.

I show her the address in North Berkeley.

I'll be here if you can't reach me on the phone.

She peers at the address but doesn't take it down.

Thank you, she says.

The train stops at MacArthur Station and a barefoot man with a torn T-shirt and ripped sweatpants gets into the car. He wears boots and his toes stick out of the torn leather. He smells like something spoiled, and I push back in my seat so the guy doesn't come near me, and I feel the cool damp of my own sweat, the odor of deodorant mixed with it.

The dude makes his way down the aisle, placing cards on every passenger's knee. The woman across from me looks horrified. Everyone else hides behind their cell phones. The cards have illustrations of hands fingerspelling A through Z. The woman across from me swats hers on the floor. I ignore mine. After he hands out the cards, the dude turns around and collects them, pausing with his hand out until he receives change. All I've got is the ten bucks, and I'm not giving him that. I look at the floor, as still as a mannequin, hoping like hell I don't know this guy or if I do he doesn't recognize me. Hey, Walter! I imagine him shouting and cringe at the thought.

The woman across from me shrinks in her seat as he approaches. She tries not to watch him. She stares over my shoulder out the window. When he reaches her, he pauses and then sees the card on the floor. He picks it up and snaps his fingers in her face and holds out his hand. She shivers.

No, no, I'm not interested, she says. Thank you. Go away now, please.

The dude snaps his fingers again and makes broad, wild gestures pointing to his ears. He waves his card in the lady's face, striking her nose.

Go away! she cries, and snatches the card from him and throws it on the floor. Now go! she shouts again, squirming into a corner of her seat. She raises her hands as if he might hit her. People watch, their eyes peering above their masks. They look pained but don't move. I don't either. I want to help her, I bet everybody does, but we all have our reasons. Mine, I don't want him to recognize me.

Leave me alone! the woman shouts.

The train jolts and slows to a stop at the North Berkeley station and the dude stumbles to the floor. As he gets up, I step in front of him to get off. He stands and tries to lean around me, but I'm pushed up against him by other people getting off. Everyone hurries out, the woman with the dirty gutters swept up with them. The dude stares after her. Turning to me, he gives a hard look and shoves me. I push him back and he falls. I don't recognize him. I wipe my shirt where he touched me and get off before the doors close.

I see the woman walking toward a parked car and a man waves from the driver's side. The train starts again, moving slowly, picking up speed until it rushes from the station, pounding the ground. My body vibrates until it's far enough gone that the ground beneath my feet settles and I don't feel anything but my clothes sticking to me. I look at the slip of paper with the address and start walking. Mist blows in my face. The morning fog hasn't burned off this side of the bay. I wish I had a jacket.

A sharp pull on my right shoulder spins me around, and I lose my balance and fall to my knees and hit my forehead against the pavement. Everything goes dark for a minute. I press a hand against the bump already forming and close my eyes. Someone grabs my hair and jerks my head back and starts hitting my face. I throw up my hands to block the punches and then they let go and start kicking me and I roll up into a ball until they stop. I don't move. I hear my breath fast and furious. I open my eyes and raise my head and make out the figure of the dude running.

Pushing myself up, I pick the grit off my face. Blood drips from my nose onto my shirt. I feel my face swelling around my nose and under my eyes. My back and ribs ache. A breeze picks up my fallen mask and swirls it away. After a moment, I stand, holding my head. Dizzy, I sit back down. I piss myself. I smell it.

Looking out at the street, I see the lady from the train staring at me, a hand over her mouth. The guy she met watches me too, as he talks into a cell phone. I stand again and wobble forward, arms out for balance.

Everything was fine until it wasn't. Oscar was right. I shouldn't have taken a shower. I'd've caught an earlier train and this wouldn't have happened.

Someone yells, Wait! and I see the woman wave at me and I cover my mouth so she doesn't see my teeth, not that it matters now. The man with her points to a police car and an ambulance racing toward the parking lot. I keep walking. There's a liquor store I know on University Avenue and Sacramento Street. A long walk but not too long. I stop at a drinking fountain and rinse my face. The cuts sting. I finger my nose, wincing. More blood drips onto my shirt. I tilt my head back to stop the bleeding, stare into a gray sky.

I'll have to get another change of clothes.

When I see Oscar again.

Oscar

She knocks.

I look up from my desk. Walter has just left. She doesn't move, stands by the open door to my office, sucks on her lower lip. I wait, take her in. High cheekbones, loose-fitting jeans torn at the knee. Tits just so, pressed against her T-shirt. About my age, I'm guessing. Mid, late thirties—something like that. A red welt on her arm, a cut on her swollen chin. Right cheek is swollen too. She wears makeup, not much though, perhaps to hide the bruised cheek. A blue scarf covers her blond hair.

Whatever happened, she put some time into herself before coming here. She has pride. I like that. It means either she doesn't know what this place is or she does and wants everyone to know she's different. That she doesn't belong here. I want her. The thought, more of a conclusion really, comes to me just like that. I want her. I'll do her. She's mine. That's how I roll. I think of the couple who walked in last month. What was the wife's name?

Yes? I say.

She hesitates. My desk faces the wall. When I turn toward the door, I face her. I have arranged my office in accordance with social services psycho-babble bullshit drilled into me at in-service trainings. Your desk should not stand between you and the client. No barriers. Don't cross your legs or fold your arms across your chest. Hands on your knees. Be open, accessible. Appear as vulnerable as the client. Instill trust.

People get paid to dream this nonsense up. I deal with the crap and turn it to my advantage. The trainings provide a day off more or less without cutting into my vacay time. Sign in, hang out until the first break, split, and go home. Nobody notices. I spend maybe two hours at the training and then take the rest of the day off.

What are you? Like a social worker, right? she asks. Her voice is soft, a little hoarse. I like its rough edges.

Benefits advocate, I say. Basically the same thing as a social worker. More or less.

I called a help hotline. They told me to come here.

I see. What's going on?

I watch her step into my office, staying close to the wall until she reaches a chair and sinks into it. I follow her eyes as they wander the bare walls, my cluttered desk, the pile of trash bags in a corner filled with donated clothing I've yet to sort. I flip a switch, turn on a ceiling fan. I keep the windows closed and my office gets stuffy. If I opened them, I'd smell the piss on the sidewalk from the night before and the spilled garbage scattered by dogs.

My office opens to the drop-in center where people with no other place to go hang out playing cards and sleeping during the day, heads on the tables or sometimes stretched out on the floor. Three alcoholism counselors stand around desks in back. They check clients into a second-floor detox. If they're too drunk to make it up the stairs, they're put on exercise mats near the intake desks. I notice Katie come in through a rear door. She punches a clock with her time card. She normally works the swing shift but she's in early. Maybe someone on the morning shift had to leave.

Katie. I like her. I could have her. But she has a job, a place to live. She doesn't need me. No, I have no need for her.

I think I need a place to stay, the woman says.

You think?

I do.

I look at the clock. Eleven. The day already feels long. I started at eight. Caught the N Judah train from my apartment in the Richmond district, the morning fog off the Bay still heavy as a blanket. It will be just as heavy when I go home. I'd like to move to the Mission. Not nearly so much fog. But the Richmond's out of the way. I rarely run into any clients and coworkers there. The gray drab of the fog keeps everyone inside. What happens in the Richmond stays in the Richmond.

Looking at the woman, I'm glad it's been a slow morning. Walter and just one or two others before him. I just finished giving a guy a letter to get on general assistance. To receive GA, the city's lingo for welfare, you have to show you have a place to live. The city requires a receipt from a landlord. However, to get a receipt you need the GA check first to pay for a place. No check, no place. No receipt, no check. The proverbial catch-22. Smoke and mirrors to deny welfare and save money. Crazy right?

I think so too. I got tired of telling clients there was nothing I could do. The city's rules. I'm helpless, whine, whine, whine. Fuck that. That's not how I roll. No, I came up with a plan, ingenious when I think about it. No one else, not the benefits advocate before me or the guy before that one, thought of it. I did.

I love telling this story. Here's what I do: I type To whom it may concern on Fresh Start letterhead to the DSS. This letter, I write, is confirmation that so and so has a room at one of the residential hotels in the Tenderloin. Please facilitate his GA application so he may continue paying rent blah, blah, blah.

The DSS doesn't ask questions, doesn't challenge me. It just needs the paper, some kind of bogus documentation that the client is spending the welfare check on housing. The client gets the check and may use it for rent, booze, or both. That's not my concern. I get my clients their GA checks. I keep them off the street for a night, or at least I give them that option. I beat the system. I accept the gratitude of my clients. I care. That's how I roll.

I might have missed this woman had it been a busy morning. She might not have waited for me. It's the first of the month, which is always kind of a slow time. Mother's Day, the clients call it. The DSS issues welfare checks on the first and the fifteenth of every month and men emerge from nowhere to lay claim to women with dependent children who receive cash grants and food stamps. I see the women later, broke usually and sometimes beat up, sometimes kicked out of their apartment with or without their kids. I wonder if that's her story. Part of it anyway.

You mean you need shelter? I say to her.

She nods yes.

OK. Any children?

No.

Good, I think. I don't take women home who have kids. Gets a little complicated with kids. I rummage in my desk for a shelter directory.

We have a shelter here but it's just for men.

She doesn't respond.

That doesn't mean I can't help you, I say.

She has all her teeth. Funny the things I notice. But teeth are a plus. Most of my clients don't have teeth or the few they do have stand alone in their mouths like rotted stumps, brown and chipped, ready to dissolve into what's left of their gums. Their fingers, too, are often stained from rolling cigarettes. Her fingers look as pale as mushroom stems.

She stands out as much as that woman and her husband I saw last month. The husband wore black slacks, a pressed shirt, and dark tie as if he thought some sort of formality was involved in asking for help. At first, I thought he was dropping off a donation. His wife stuck close to his side and I caught a whiff of her perfume. She looked anxious, as if she had not slept. Her clothes fit her well. She was put together, flat stomach, slim hips, full mouth with red lipstick. I imagined touching her neck.

Her husband held a referral slip like it meant something. He took out a pair of reading glasses, read it, and handed it to me: Needs housing, someone had scrawled across it. The man explained he had been a chef at a Marina District restaurant, someplace I'd never heard of, when an earthquake damaged the building beyond repair and he lost his job. She had been a bank teller but got laid off about the same time. They resorted to temp agencies but found little work. After they lost their apartment they stayed with friends. It was a friend who suggested they go to the DSS for help. Someone there sent them to Fresh Start.

We don't belong here, the husband said.

But you're here, I replied.

They looked at the floor. Outside my office, men and women in clothes that hadn't seen a washer in days, reeking of their own fetidness and the smoke from campfires they had passed out beside in Golden Gate Park stood waiting to be let into the drop-in center. They raised their voices above one another and got louder and louder until the words collapsed from the weight of their own volume into a tumult of senseless noise made even louder by the spacious building that had once been a warehouse and now served as an echo chamber to all the racket. The husband and wife stared at me bewildered by all the commotion.

Do you have a place to go tonight?

No. But we're not homeless, not in that way.

In what way are you homeless?

The husband didn't answer. His wife glanced at the ceiling and held a hand up against the lights. I smiled understandingly. It was a smile that reassured and prodded shy smiles from them in return, because to them it meant what they wanted it to mean: Things would work out. Things would be fine. It told them they mattered, but to believe this they had to believe in me, to give up a part of themselves to me and be led into the unknown. To be dominated, as I liked to think of it. I mattered, not them. To be sitting in my office meant they no longer existed as anything more than my clients, whom I would do with as I pleased. For their benefit or my pleasure. Sometimes both, but not often. My choice in any case. I held my smile just long enough to provide temporary comfort before I dragged a hand across my mouth and wiped it from my face and the ambiguity of their situation returned and they stood looking at me, a man they did not know but wanted to trust, who did not appear to be all that different from themselves, but who, without my smile, conveyed no thought or feeling at all. Be a mystery, I told myself, and exert control.

`After a moment, I explained to them that I could give them shelter. By shelter I meant an army cot and a blanket. However, I would have to refer the wife to a woman's shelter. If they had a child, I could refer them both to a family shelter. Without a child, however, they would have to split up.

Men and women sleeping together—it gets complicated, you understand, I said. Of course, if you want to stay together, I can refer you to a residential hotel. By hotel, I mean a room in a run-down building in the Tenderloin or on Sixth south of Market. Do you know Sixth Street? It's skid row. We're not talking Marriott, just so you understand.

I think someone made a mistake, the husband said. I don't think they meant to send us here. They gave us the wrong referral.

I did not ask who that someone was. Some bureaucrat under the illusion that a nonprofit social services agency could help where the feds, state, and city could not or would not. I didn't tell them they were too late, that they were no longer deserving of help. Not once they reached this level. They were down now with the bad people: drunks, junkies, hookers, those homeless men and women who had been on the street for years and lived off soup kitchens and shelters and the stamina of their abused bodies. The ones stepped over and ignored. That's who came to me. That's who they were now.

Mistake or not, that's what I can do for you, I said.

We'll take a hotel, the husband said.

I gave them a seven-day referral to a dive on Eddy. I stood and shook their hands. I held onto the woman's hand and squeezed her fingers before I let go, and she pulled her hand away but not quickly, and she gave me a searching look and he returned her look.

I saw the couple the next morning. The husband still wore his tie and slacks. Her hair was pulled back and looked as if it had not been combed. Their clothes were not as crisp as the day before. Perhaps they had dressed in a hurry and did not pause long enough to pat out the wrinkles. Or maybe they slept in them, huddled together, frightened. The hotel, they told me, disgusted them. Rats, broken toilets, filthy mattresses, no sheets or blankets. How could it even be called a hotel?

I tried to warn you, I said.

The couple returned to the hotel and stayed for the length of their referral. They stopped by my office day after day looking a little more haggard each time. I gave them referrals to soup kitchens and a Salvation Army jobs counselor. The husband stopped wearing his tie. His wife kept her hair pulled back but it was clear to the benefits advocate that she was no longer washing it. Circles pooled beneath her eyes, and lines I had not noticed before stretched out from around her mouth, thinner without lipstick. When their time at the hotel was finished, they asked to stay in a shelter.

You'll have to split up, I reminded them.

We understand, the man said.

I gave the man a bed ticket for the Fresh Start night shelter. The line to get in starts at five, I told him. First come, first served. I then made some calls to three women's shelters. I asked the first two if they had space. They did. I thanked them and hung up without reserving a bed. The third shelter, Randolph House in the Haight, was full. That's what I wanted to hear. I got off the phone, wrote her a referral, and gave it to her with a bus token.

The number nine bus will drop you almost at the door, I explained. You catch it at Market and Van Ness Avenue. You should leave here about five.

She and her husband thanked me. They left my office and sat in the drop-in center like two people in a doctor's waiting room. They asked me for something to read, but I had nothing. They shifted their chairs away from two drunken men arguing over a pinochle game, toward other men who staggered and shouted at the walls. I let them use the staff restroom so they would not have to deal with the vomit and the clogged toilets in the one in the drop-in. Sometimes, the wife asked to sit in my office. The husband stayed in the drop-in, and I wondered if he was trying to prove something to himself. That he could handle it. Take it. Did he think he was being strong for her? His wife watched me dispense bus tokens and write letters for GA applicants. I glanced at her off and on and concluded that if she was not comfortable, she at least felt safe with me. My office. My domain. She had left her husband to sit beside me, her protector.

It's a pleasant memory, but I cannot linger on it. I have another woman in my office, the one who came in after Walter. She is waiting for me to help her. She needs me now.

I'll make some calls to women's shelters, I tell her.

Will I get in one?

We'll see. A lot of people got their checks today so shelters should not be as full. But you never know.

She stares out a window at Leavenworth Street and crosses her arms. Her T-shirt rides down one shoulder, and I notice pale purple bruises before she tugs it back up without looking at me.

There's this place in the Haight, I tell her. Randolph House. I can't promise they'll have space. It depends how long they're letting people stay. It only has ten beds. But it would get you out off the street.

OK.

I call and get a recording: If you're calling about shelter, press three. Another recording: The shelter is full at this time. Leave your name after the beep and you'll be put on a waiting list. If a space opens, someone will call you.

Hello, I'm the benefits advocate at Fresh Start, I say, talking as if there is a real person on the other end. I have a client who needs a bed.

I pause, pretend to be listening.

Will do, I say after a moment. Thanks for your time.

I hang up.

They won't know if they'll have a bed until later. I'll call back.

I hold out hope, wanting her to see me making an effort. A nice man trying to help. Earn her appreciation. Wear her down with the waiting, the calls, the worry. Increase her dependency.

Thank you, she says.

I worked it the same way with the man and his wife. He got in line for the shelter and she prepared to leave for Randolph House. She and her husband looked at each other. They held hands and stood for a long time facing each other. Then she let go of his fingers and walked out of the drop-in looking very small. I watched her go, entered two shelter referrals on the stat form in my computer and clicked save.

I waited about ten minutes to give her time to reach Market and Van Ness. Then I grabbed a red marker, locked my office, and got in my car. Prostitutes lingered outside. I sized them up but wanted nothing to do with them. I drove down Larkin to Market and hung a right until I reached Van Ness. I saw her standing off to one side from a huddle of people beneath a bus shelter, her back turned against a hard-blowing, damp wind. I beeped and beeped again until she looked up. She looked confused and then she recognized me and hurried over. I rolled down the passenger door window and was about to say, I got off early. I'm headed home, and live that way. Let me give you a ride, but she opened the door without question and got in.

I hope it's that easy with this woman here. As she waits to leave for Randolph House, I bide my time by collecting loose pens and markers on my desk, gathering them in a bunch, and brushing them in a drawer.

Housekeeping, I tell her.

I consider the drawer and decide to take a blue marker with me. The color of her headscarf. I will draw a line on my bedroom door, a notch of sorts to indicate I had her. I used a red marker for the husband's wife, red to remind me of her full mouth.

I watch a bus drone past my office window. An old man sits in the doorway of a closed thrift store across the street. Fog stretches across the top of the store, thick fingers of it breaking and twisting.

Hey, you got any bus tokens? Katie asks me, poking her head through my door. I got a guy I need to send to General.

She notices the woman and drags a finger over the woman's swollen chin. The woman pulls away. Her eyes tear up.

You all right, honey? Katie asks the woman.

Here, I say, giving Katie a token.

She takes it and gives a slight jerk of her head toward the door. I get up and follow her out. The woman turns slightly in her chair to make room for me to pass her and my hand brushes against her shoulder. She flinches.

Where're you going?

To get more bus tokens, I tell her.

I let my fingers linger against her shirt. She stiffens but doesn't move. I close the door behind me.

What are you doing for her? Katie asks.

Shelter.

Looks like she needs more than shelter.

That's all she asked for.

Look at her, Katie says. Those aren't birthmarks on her face. If a man did that to her, she's not going to talk to you.

I don't appreciate her tone. A little pushy. A little forgetting herself.

I'm just saying you might need some help on this one, Katie says. She might not open up to you.

She will. She has.

Katie shakes her head. I watch her walk away and go back into my office.

Sorry to keep you waiting.

It's OK.

I sit back at my desk.

Let's try Randolph House again.

She taps her foot against the floor as I dial.

It'll be fine, I tell her in a voice I know sounds soothing, calm.

She nods, says nothing.

They get that way after a while, get quiet. The uncertainty. What's there to say? The man's wife had been quiet in my car after she got in, and I didn't speak, so that she would know I was comfortable with her silence. I parked across the street from Randolph House and walked her inside to the reception desk. The sound of dozens of women's voices rushed us in a rising chorus of shouts and demands. Dirty blankets filled a cart, smelling of the women who had used them. Steam rolled across the ceiling from a shower room and the weight of it pressed against my face. A woman wrapped only in a towel ran past us, grabbed another woman by her hair, and screamed at her for taking her shampoo. Her towel fell away and they fought naked, rolling on the floor, pale wet flesh flopping and slapping the tiles. The receptionist tried to break it up but slipped on the towel and fell cursing.

The wife reached for my hand.

I can't stay here, she said.

I had not expected this level of chaos. I had presumed we'd make it to the desk and the receptionist would turn us away. Sorry, we're full. I would have pushed back, said that I was the benefits advocate for Fresh Start, that I had called and been promised a bed for my client. I would have put up a good fight all for show, of course, and then walked out with her. But this was better. Fewer theatrics. On my end, anyway.

She followed me to my car and got in. I looked at my watch. Her husband had probably been assigned a cot by now. I turned the ignition key and flipped on my headlights and drove through the fog to Lincoln Way. The trees in Golden Gate Park loomed in the mist. I turned onto Twelfth Avenue, drove three blocks and parked. She did not ask where we were going.

I live there, I said and pointed.

She looked out her window at the peeling yellow paint of my apartment building and then turned to me, and I stared back at her and kissed her on the mouth, my eyes open. She didn't move, didn't close her eyes either. I looked hard at her, pulled away, and continued looking at her. She shook her head, opened her mouth. Her hands fluttered on either side of her face and words caught in her throat as if she was trying to say something that was beyond her abilities of speech. She glanced up and down the empty street, at the quiet houses. She didn't move. She looked at me once more, eyes red. I worried she might ask for her husband, but she didn't. Her husband was equally helpless, equally alone and desperate and far away. Lost and tired, I thought. Lost and tired.

The thinking necessary to bring her to this point had entertained me, kept my mind in motion, every second belonging to itself and whatever occurred within it either informed the next or did not, but now she was broken, defeated. I had only to finish a game that had already ended. I felt bored. I watched her open her door, get out, and wait. I felt for the red marker in my pocket. I opened my door. Neither of us spoke as we walked up the steps, our silence a pact so solitary in its understanding of her limited options that we both knew there was nothing more to be said.

Now I am involved with another woman, another game. I anticipate a similar ending. I call Randolph House and get the same recording.

If you're . . .

Hello, yes, I called earlier from Fresh Start about a bed for my client. You have a bed?

. . . press three.

That's great, thank you. I'll send her over.

I hang up. I expect that Randolph House will be calmer this time. That's fine. I know what to say.

Randolph has a bed, I tell her. Took a while but it was worth the wait.

I flash her a quick reassuring smile. I expect her to look relieved. Instead, she crosses her arms and stares at the floor.

What's wrong? I ask.

May I see the woman who was just here?

Katie?

Is that her name?

Yes. Why?

I just want to. I liked her. Can't I?

Of course. Sure, you can, but it would be a mistake. You need to go to Randolph House now or you'll lose your bed.

I'll go, but I want to see Katie first.

Her voice rises, cracks. Nervous but insistent. Almost annoyed. At me. My mind goes blank. I don't know what to say.

Just go to the shelter, I insist. I try not to sound angry, control the tone of my voice.

She stands.

Where're you going?

To see her. Katie.

She walks out the door.

Wait.

She turns to me. A determined stare. I drum my fingers against my desk. She doesn't move. She's already gone. I've lost her.

The other woman, the man's wife, she did as I told her. Tears inside my apartment but no questions. I wonder where she went after she left the next morning. Did she meet her husband? I assume she did, assume she told him nothing. I didn't expect to see them again and I didn't. Where did they go? Maybe it worked out for them; maybe it didn't.

Just a minute, I say again. Wait here.

I stand, walk past her and into the drop-in. A missed opportunity. It happens. I imagine her staring after me and regretting her decision. Too late. I reject her. That's how I roll.

I stop at Katie's desk. A woman sits beside her. Circles of pink rouge make the woman's pale, tense face look even paler.

My client wants to speak with you, I say.

Oh?

I'll send her over.

I'm doing an intake.

I look at her client. She stares straight ahead. Thirtyish. She smells of cigarettes. But the way her straw-colored hair trails down to the small of her back interlaced in one long braid appeals to me. She spent a little time on herself making that braid.

Take my client, I say. I'll finish here for you.

Tom

I look at my watch. Five o'clock. I've been at work since seven. I'm expecting a call from the mayor's office. Probably too late, city offices are closed by now, but I'll give it a few more minutes. I go over my staff list and have barely begun going through it when the reception desk phone rings. I jump in anticipation.

A call for you, Tom, Jay shouts.

Send it through.

Jay patches the call to my phone.

Fresh Start, may I help you? I say. You want to donate clothes? Well, just bring them down. Park behind the building and ring the bell. Thank you for thinking of the homeless. Have a good day.

I hang up.

We don't need more clothes, we've got tons, but if someone gives you pants and shirts one day, they might give you a check the next. So I accept their stuff. After they drop it off, I'll ask a volunteer to take it to the Salvation Army. Our clothes closet is full. I could use underwear and socks, but those things rarely get donated. I think people would feel self-conscious giving away their old underwear. I get it. It'd be weird. So buy some and donate new underwear. No one does that, or at least very few. They'll write me a check. But ask them to buy new clothes and give them to me, no way. Doesn't happen.

I pick up the staff list again.

The California State Assembly and governor agreed on a

budget last night that will slash social services statewide. The cuts will be passed on to cities. Our mayor will make noise about trying to absorb them, how he'll lobby the governor. Some years he means it. Sometimes it helps but not much. A few thousand dollars saved here and there. Not enough. Never enough to avoid deep cuts of some kind. Once all the posturing is out of the way, social service providers like me with city contracts will get a call from the mayor's homeless coordinator. He'll tell each of us how much our budgets have been reduced. I'm waiting for his call.

Budget redistribution, as the city calls it, always boils down to laying off staff, something my contract forbids. It doesn't look good for a helping agency that hires the homeless to terminate employees. So the city passes along budget cuts but forbids me to reduce staff. However, my contract allows for transition opportunities. No one gets laid off. Instead, I transition them out. It's just words, man. I can play the game.

In the past, I've made these opportunities available to staff I thought had a good chance of finding work elsewhere, staff who had acquired some education before their addictions consumed them, who had at least a minimal work history that preceded their time with me. Last year, I transitioned Shelley, our alcoholism counselor. She has a master's degree in sociology and was more than qualified for the position, but she showed little initiative and spent most of her time on her phone chatting with friends. Faced with budget cuts, I eliminated her position. She took it hard. I lied and told her it had nothing to do with her job performance. That it was solely a budgetary decision. Dollars and cents. I had to cut somewhere. I didn't see the point of scolding her for her lackadaisical attitude. Frankly, she could have been God's gift, but because she was one of my higher-paid staff I probably would have cut her anyway. I heard she got married and has a kid on the way. That's good. That's nice. I'm glad she's doing all right. I wish I had a few more like her. But after years of transition opportunities, I'm pretty much out of people like Shelley. I'm left with staff who have been homeless, some of them for years. They have problems, ongoing mental health and other issues that mean they won't enter the traditional workforce anytime soon. Only another social services agency would hire them, but the directors of those programs are doing what I'm doing: cutting staff.

My program coordinator, Don, walks into the office. He calls himself codirector because I include him in decision-making. Some people are like that; their job title means everything and codirector sounds better to him, I suppose, than program coordinator. It's about power, prestige, some need for his self-esteem, but he's not my equal. On the staff flowchart his name is right below mine and he knows it. We all answer to somebody and he answers to me. I'm not heavy with it. I don't lord it over him or anyone. But I am the director. Just saying.

I get up, pace around my office, sit down again. I wish the mayor's office would call. I want to know what I'll have to do, how deep I have to cut. It won't make it any easier, but at least I'd know and could get it over with, crunch the numbers, who stays, who goes. Hired one year, gone the next. That's how it works. Fired, laid-off, transitioned, it doesn't matter what you call it. It's all the same, someone's out of a job. The look in their eyes. The sense of betrayal. The tears. All the self-respect they had clawed back into their lives after years of screwing up—or maybe not screwing up but just experiencing bad luck—gone in the two or three sentences it takes me to tell them they're out of job. What will they have left? A room at a residential hotel they will no longer be able to afford, a tab at a convenience store they will no longer be able to pay, a mirror over a sink they'll no longer want to look at, that's what. I'll see them back on the street in no time, back to passed out on the sidewalks and in doorways or asleep in our homeless shelter, back in line at the DSS applying for whatever benefit they might be eligible for, and they'll be back the next day and the day after that until it's time to return to the shelter, a homeless person's version of nine to five, an indistinguishable mass of men and women in ill-fitting thrift-store clothes, as if they'd never been employed by me or anyone. As if standing in line and sleeping in a shelter had always been their life. After a while, it probably feels that way.

I look at my staff list and pause at Don's name. He could easily get another job. College educated, master's degrees in theology and sociology. Never been homeless. He lives as middle-class an existence as I do. I like him. More than that it helps having someone in charge when I'm out of the building, but now I have to decide whether to keep him or cut him so another staff person less likely to find another job can stay. Everyone's expendable. Don understands that. Or he will.

Jay's phone rings again and he transfers the call to me. As I pick up the receiver, Don lights a smoke and takes the staff list from me. After a moment, I hang up.

More clothing donations, I say.

He thrusts the list at me.

You marked my name?

Just an ink mark, Don. I was counting the number of staff with my pen, how we can combine positions to make up for any staff cuts. I've made no decisions.

I haven't. I'm not lying but there's no point saying I'm thinking of eliminating your position either. At least not until I know what's what. No point adding to the stress. I'm not trying to torture people. And I was counting. How do we stay open twenty-four hours with fewer staff? How do I pick up the slack? Ask those who remain to work overtime? I don't have the money for that.

Who do I need? How much will I save if I cut this person and that person? I have to give my recommendations to McGraw after we get the call. He'll examine my numbers, see if they add up. The bottom line is the bottom line, he likes to say. It is what it is, no more, no less. It's not my fault; I remind myself of that.

I know you have to consider everybody, Don says.

I was just counting, I say again.

Don is a recovering alcoholic and is HIV positive. He recently applied for an administrative position with the AIDS Foundation. He's one of three finalists. The foundation's director told him he would decide by the end of today. I hope they offer him the job. I'd miss him, but it would allow me to cut a position without any pain.

Don doesn't appear sick. He's thin, as thin as he was three years ago when I interviewed him for program coordinator. He came in late his first day at work, circles under his eyes, unshaven, not a great way for a new employee to make an impression. He said his alarm didn't go off, but I wondered if he'd had a slip and begun drinking again. But he was alert, didn't smell of booze, and he was never late again. That night on Don's way home, a mugger jumped him, held a knife to his back and demanded his wallet. One of his new business cards fell out of his pocket and the mugger picked it up. When he saw that Don worked at Fresh Start, he apologized and returned the wallet. He had crashed in our shelter several times, he said. He asked for a clothing referral. Don told him to come in the next morning. The mugger didn't make an issue of it. He apologized again and walked away. Even a mugger understood the importance of this place, Don told me the next day. He was impressed. I have to say I was too. Not with the mugger but with Don. Had I been him, I'd've quit, called in, That's it, I'm done.

What's funny? Don asks.

I was just thinking of your first day at work. That night you got mugged.

He smirks.

Feels like a long time ago.

Ever see him again? I ask.

Don shakes his head.

Not that I know of. I don't think he came in for the clothing referral.

You'd know, I say. I'd have given him his clothing referral just for having the balls to come in.

And then eighty-six him for carrying a weapon.

We laugh. We get along. I'll be sorry to see him go. During the week, we take our lunch breaks together and sometimes catch a movie after work. We watch each other's cats when one of us goes on vacation. I'd feed his cat on the way home from work and sit in his living room and listen to it eat. I imagined what it was like to be him. Getting up in the morning and slipping into the designer jeans he liked to wear. Tucking in his shirt and tying his shoes. Going out the door. What did he think at those moments? What were his thoughts about going to the job and working for me?

Last December, Don and I spent a weekend afternoon at his house, writing Christmas cards to our staff. Fresh Start's budget did not have money for a holiday bonus, so we decided personal handwritten notes that we each signed would at least show how much we appreciate them. Don and I sat on the floor with cards and envelopes strewn at our feet, sunlight cutting through the blinds, and dividing the task between us.

I'll write the notes to the paid staff; you take the volunteers, I said.

Aren't we both writing notes to everyone?

That would take forever. You take volunteers and I'll take staff.

Why don't we split them? Half volunteers, half staff. Each of us.

No.

Why?

The paid staff need to hear from me, because I'm the one who told them there would be no bonus this year. You get the volunteers. They weren't expecting anything, not even a card.

I picked out one showing Santa Claus scrambling down a chimney, a huge stuffed sack thrown over one shoulder. Smiling reindeer stood with him on the snow-covered rooftop. Don stood up and went into the kitchen. He opened a cabinet and took out a glass and filled it with Pepsi. He drank by the kitchen sink without offering me anything. I opened the card and wrote Dear Don. It was all so petty, really, when I think about it. Except Don has something over me. Or he may believe he does.

I have a habit of stopping by the Comeback Club for a beer on my way home. One afternoon, Don came in. The door was open to the sidewalk and he walked inside through a stream of sunlight. He gave the bartender two dollars and got change. Maybe he needed it for the bus. I was at a table, waiting to order a beer and a sandwich. Don did a double-take when he saw me. I avoided his gaze but watched him without looking at him directly. He left without a word. I wondered why he was there. He could get change anywhere. Maybe he'd been chipping all this time and I never knew. Maybe he was planning to buy a drink before he saw me. He thought quickly, changed course, got change. Smooth. With his diagnosis, he has good reason to drink. Just saying. If he's slipping and chipping I got another reason to let him go. Not that I need one but it would make it easier if he doesn't get the AIDS Foundation gig. It's all about the numbers. Friendship can have no place in my thinking.

Jay's phone rings.

For you, Tom, Jay shouts, and transfers the call.

A Salvation Army counselor asks me if we have spare bus tokens. I tell her I'm tapped out. Don and I agreed a long time ago to give out just five tokens a day. Otherwise we'd go through them too fast. And still we have none left.

Ginger, one of my floor supervisors, pokes her head into my office.

Nothing, I say when I hang up. It wasn't them.

She sighs and asks for the key to the printer to photocopy her stats. I give it to her. I don't often let staff use the copy machine. Our clients need to make copies of their birth certificates, Social Security cards, and IDs for various benefits applications, I get it, but I tell them to go elsewhere so we can save money on paper.

What do you think? Ginger asks.

That I won't know until I get the call.

Two years ago, Ginger was on the street. We helped her with shelter. When one of my staff noticed her talking to herself we sent her to San Francisco General for a mental health eval. She was diagnosed with schizophrenia. We helped her get on disability so she could get the medication she needs. She stopped hearing voices and a social worker at General helped enroll her in a job-training program that allowed her to remain eligible for disability for one year from her hire date if the job didn't work out. The program covered her salary and I hired her. Tomorrow will mark her one-year anniversary. She knows I know that she can get back on disability if I cut her.

The reception desk phone rings. Jay sends it through.

Fresh Start, may I help you?

An Episcopal Sanctuary volunteer asks me if I have bus tokens. One of his clients needs a ride to Walgreens to fill a prescription.

Sorry, I say, I don't.

Ginger looks through the door.

It wasn't them, I tell her.

She makes a face, turns away from me. I hear her mutter something to herself and then cover her mouth. She looks at the floor. Her cheeks twitch and she hurries back to her office. Last year she organized a staff Christmas party at her apartment. I went and I'll never forget the raw, acidic stink rising out of her bathtub when I used her bathroom. Parting the shower curtain, I saw kitty litter and cat shit. I pulled the shower curtain closed.

It looks like the cat has been using your tub, I told Ginger. I just thought you should know.

She stared at me with a reproachful look.

Why were you in my bathroom? she snapped. You should have asked.

I'm sorry, I told her.

She hurried away and shut the bathroom door and stood in front of it with her arms crossed over her chest, glaring. Even when Ginger had it together, cracks showed. I never did see a cat.

Jay's phone rings. He points a finger at me like a conductor singling out a member of the orchestra. I pick up.

Fresh Start, may I help you?

Another request for a bus token. Somebody trying to get to a detox outside the city. They'll sell the token and buy a drink, I'm sure. But I'm tired of saying no. I shout to Ginger, tell her to leave a token at the front desk.

I go over my staff list again and put a question mark by her name. Then I cross it out and draw a line through her name. We'll get cut. I don't know how much yet but we'll get cut. I have to make choices.

So sad, Don says watching me. So sad.

I ignore him, glance outside. A closed sign hangs in the window of the restaurant across the street. The owner makes killer hamburgers. Because we're across the street, he allows my guys credit. When they don't pay, he complains to me. I have told him time and time again not to do that. I say, you're dealing with people who haven't worked in a long time. They're not used to handling money. They don't make much. My guys probably have racked up over a hundred bucks charging food. He didn't listen. Now, he expects me to pay. Maybe I should cut the staff who owe him, stop this before it gets further out of hand.

Don rolls his cell phone in his hand. I hear him tap, tap, tap it against the desk.

Well, he says, speaking as if he's in the middle of a thought, I'll miss you.

Where're you going?

I mean if I get the job at the AIDS Foundation. Or if you lay me off.

I won't lay you off, I tell him and instantly regret saying it. I will if I have to. He knows it too. Maybe that's a good thing, I don't know.

Don gets up and tells Jay to take a break. Jay pushes out of his chair, hesitates, and then sits down again. He leans back, chair tipped against the wall.

Go on, Don says.

Where should I go? Jay says.

Nowhere if you don't want, Don says.

You have a cigarette?

Here, Don says and offers him one.

Jay takes it and stands off to one side. Don sits at the desk. He looks at me and then turns to the phone. He rests his hand on the receiver as if he anticipates it will ring at any moment. Ginger and Jay watch him. Ginger presses a hand to her chest and mutters something to herself. I just want to go home. If the call comes, I hope neither Don nor Jay answers. Let it ring. Ring all night if need be. I already know what I have to do. It's all the same, no matter what they tell me. I just go with the numbers.

Keith

I drop a plastic bag on the picnic table and sit across from Jay.
A few guys wander around the grass in blue VA hospital robes
and stop to listen to the cars on Clement Street. Trees muffle the
noise, although you can still faintly hear the cars like something
far away. The grounds slope up to a crowded parking lot, and I
see some older guys in the shade wearing sunglasses and sitting
in wheelchairs beneath trees with canes across their laps, waiting
for what, I don't know. A ride, probably.

Jay, ice cream and cookies after the AA meeting, this guy says,
stopping by our table. He leans on a walker and bums a smoke
off me. Nicotine stains his gray beard, and his hospital gown
slips off one shoulder and gauze pads cover spots on his thin
arms where a nurse might've stuck him with an IV.

When's the meeting? Jay asks.

In an hour.

OK.

You'll remember?

I'll try.

Jay sips some coffee and watches the guy walk away with a
thousand-yard stare that sees through him and beyond to places
I cannot imagine. I take two cellophane-wrapped packages out
of my coat pocket and slide them toward him.

I brought you fudge grahams too, I say, pointing to the plastic
bag, and some fruit-flavored wafers.

How'd you find me?

The nurse from the ninth floor told me you were out here.

When I returned from Iraq to San Francisco, I fucking drank. Anniversary of an attack, I drank; anniversary of a buddy's death, I drank. I fucking hung out with homeless Vietnam vets on Sixth Street. Man, I hid a lot behind the bottle. I put the bottle up only when Katherine threatened to leave me. I came here to the ninth floor, the psych wing of the VA, for two weeks and dried out. I still wasn't right. I was still forgetting shit but I wasn't drinking, which made the forgetting that much harder to take. But I didn't know it was a problem. Not at first. I was just glad to be home and out of the VA. During those two weeks on the ninth floor, Katherine would visit me once a day. She brought bags of chocolate chip cookies. She liked to bake cookies, but these were store-bought. Said she didn't have time to bake. Should have known then she was already gone.

Got some Twizzlers here too in the bag.

All right.

I open a package of pink-colored wafers and bite into one. The crunching noise fills my head like breaking glass. I want to ask Jay how he's doing but decide to leave it alone. The way my brain is, I'd probably forget what the fuck he said anyway.

I like the strawberry wafers. You ought to try one, Jay.

OK.

I watch him take one, wondering if I'll forget I was here when I go home.

In Iraq, we used to give Skittles to the kids of hajis building our bunkers. You have Skittles when you were there?

No, I say.

None of those haji kids were bad. I don't hold anything against them, Jay says. They just see their daddies fighting all the time and do like them.

I didn't deal much with kids over there. They lined the road sometimes when we went out on patrol. They'd throw rocks at us, tink, tink, tink against the vic. Just when I'd think, fuck it, it's only rocks, one of them would chuck a grenade and the explosion would toss us around like bowling pins, not hurt so much as pretty goddamned roughed up.

We had a guard tower. Tower Three. This kid and his mother lived right outside the tower in the middle of the line of fire. I'm talking snipers and mortars, and they lived with it day in and day out like people in Seattle who say, It ain't nothing, all this rain.

I mean they didn't have armor or a weapon of any kind. Nothing that I knew of. I don't know how they made it. The kid was small. He had a narrow face, black hair. Maybe thirteen, fourteen. One round in him and he'd've busted in half. His mother was dressed in black. All you could see was her eyes, like some ninja warrior. They never acknowledged us. The kid threw rocks. Not at us. Just liked to throw rocks. I got to wondering, though, whose side were he and his mother on? Do they lay IEDs? Fuck rules of engagement, why hadn't we wasted them?

Jay is a hell of a lot more generous than I am. Do like their daddies do. Shit, the way I see it, hajis aren't people. They're fucking hajis. That's what we called them. Fucking hajis. Some nights, I watch haji-made videos on YouTube and wish I still had my weapon, the motherfuckers. I was in Target the other week, I think, the one in Oakland. I'm pretty sure it was Target, and I saw a guy, this guy with a turban. Fucking towel head. I don't go to Target now. Goddamn hajis. When you give up so much for people you don't even know and they try to kill you—did kill a shitload of us—fuck them. I don't even know what haji means. If I did, I might think differently about calling them that. I'd call them something worse if I knew something worse, but I don't.

I met Jay at a support group for Iraq War vets at Fresh Start.

The VA told me about it. Jay was short but sturdy like a Mack truck. He was eating cheese and crackers laid out on the snack table like he'd never get enough. We didn't say much beyond, Hey, brother, how's it going? I'm Keith. I'm Jay. He spoke slowly, his mouth full of cheese and crackers, and I pulled up a chair. He told me he volunteered at Fresh Start. Answered phones. What do you do? he asked me. Come here, I told him.

I got in the habit of sitting next to him at the group meetings. I like consistency. There was a morning when the newspaper delivery guy forgot our apartment. I sat by the front window and looked out the curtain to where the paper normally landed every morning at six and thought, Where is it? What's going on? Why's it late? The barking of dogs behind us on Sixteenth Avenue alerted me that something was wrong. Then the dogs stopped and the quiet was worse. This guy Perez shot dogs all the time, these huge Cujo-looking things. He shot one right in the mouth. This haji farmer came out, asked what we were going to do for his injured dog. I took out my KA-BAR and cut its throat. There's your fucking dog, I said.

But the paper wasn't there and Perez wasn't with me. I stared out the window, watched the gray morning sky turn to light blue, and wondered which side of the street would have the ambush. Sparrows flew out of trees. What had frightened them? I felt like I could breathe and breathe and never get enough air. I refused to leave the apartment, refused to leave the window. Katherine got on the phone and demanded delivery of our newspaper. Not this afternoon, she shouted, now! When she brought it inside an hour later, I felt better, but then I thought, Hold up. Wait a minute. I held it in my hands afraid to move until Katherine opened it and I saw there wasn't a bomb inside.

Last week, at the Fresh Start, I didn't see Jay. That's how I lost friends in Iraq. Here on Monday morning, gone by Monday afternoon. They'd go on patrol and not come back. I lost five buddies my first week in Iraq. It was all I could do not to scream, Where the fuck is Jay?

Keith, you're looking pretty wild, Ryan, the group leader, said. What's wrong?

Where's Jay?

He's in the VA. Do you know the director here, Tom? Well, anyway, he told me that Jay got drunk and started cutting on himself in the shelter bathroom. The police had to cuff him to stop him from hurting himself.

Ryan served in Vietnam and did a prison stint when he got smashed one night on a fifth of Yukon Jack and dug a trench in his backyard. He whipshit a neighbor damn near to death after he asked Ryan a perfectly logical question: What the hell are you doing?

Suicide?

No. Cutting. Like high school kids do. Deal with the pain on the inside by hurting yourself on the outside. I think he might be bipolar.

Ryan took these psychology courses in prison, thinks he's Dr. fucking Phil now. Thinks his head's on right. That day I wanted to tell him it's not on right. That deep down in his guts he's still that fucked-up trench-digging drunk vet, and it's that guy that's going to bite him in the ass one day.

Bipolar, shit. I didn't say anything, though. I didn't. I wanted to find Jay before I forgot, and make sure I hadn't lost him.

I guess I'll go see him, I said.

After the group, I drove to the VA. I headed toward Elm Street, took a left on Turk Street and a right onto Van Ness Avenue, and then everything got dark for me and just like that I forgot where I was. I knew I'd been at the Vet Center. I knew I'd talked to Ryan. I knew I wanted to see Jay, but it was less of a plan than an idea I'd had a long time ago and that I had now just remembered. I pulled over to a 7-Eleven, bought some fudge grahams and Twizzlers and strawberry wafers and asked for directions to the VA.

I see you still have your army-issue sunglasses, Jay says.

Yeah. Want some more wafers?

Please.

I hand him a couple.

I have wacky dreams, Jay says. I see dead kids. I'm in the dream. I'm holding a .50 cal. Some are dead already. Some I'm killing. The enemy's firing from all sides, we're firing from all sides. One kid just stands there and watches me. I call him the one who got away.

Do me a favor, Jay.

What?

Next time you fall asleep, don't let him get away.

Yeah, with a .50 cal.

That'll do it. I was stationed in Balad. The C-130 carrying us in from Kuwait couldn't land—the base was being bombed. The pilot had to maneuver like a motherfucker to avoid getting hit. I saw flames below us and I thought, if an RPG nails us, that's it. A guy next to me started crying. I was shaking, felt like puking. It seemed like we circled a long time before we got the OK to land. When the doors opened, we put our heads down and ran. The guy crying got hit. Lost an arm, a hand, and both legs. He lived.

Balad was shit. Nothing but sand and heat like someone had left the oven on broil overnight and you open it in the morning and the heat blast melts your fucking face off, and dust storms and diesel exhaust that layered you brown and black, and more tanks than I'd ever seen. My unit occupied a girls school. Guys collapsed on the floor, passed out from dehydration. Mortar fire and snipers every night got them up. As soon as it got dark, that was it, the hajis opened up on us. We called the place Mortarita-ville. A real kick in the ass, I can tell you.

My third month, I was part of a supply convoy to Forward Operating Base Concord. The LT assigned me, Perez, and four other guys to Humvee soft top, double-armored, third from the rear. I rode shotgun, Smith drove. Jones, Perez, and McGuire sat in back.

We left Balad at 0800 and bounced along a wadi heavy with rocks, the land like the bottom of a dried-up, forgotten ocean with villages bleached beyond white scattered here and there but a ways off Nowheresville, Iraq.

The IED was a remote detonator mortar round. I was listening to radio traffic and Katy Perry on my iPod when, wham! my door blew the fuck open and the Humvee blasted off the ground like a rocket, dropped back down and filled with smoke so dense I couldn't see my hands. My ears rang like someone was banging pots and pans inside my head. I turned around. Jones, Perez, and McGuire glued against each other, fried black, their bodies ripped open red and spilling guts. I yelled, No! and reached for Perez and his skin came off in my hand and Smith grabbed me and hauled me out screaming. Shrapnel had totally bent the Humvee's frame, but I still had my weapon. We crawled, scrambling like snakes on the ground and shot at any-thing that moved. I was shaking, dizzy, my throat raw, my hands sticky from Perez, but I could shoot, goddamn it, I could shoot. I saw a woman walking a cow, my heart beating so hard I had a hard time breathing, and thought she had better get under that fucking cow.

She didn't. The cow blew up. Just this big fan of fucking red and the woman disappeared into it, swallowed, sucked into another dimension, gone, and I just kept firing at that spot, plowing under whatever pieces were left. We ripshit houses and trees, anything standing, anything someone might hide behind. When we stopped shooting, the sound of our breathing and thudding hearts consumed the silence and the nothingness we'd wasted.

Back at the base, I couldn't stop shaking. I puked and puked. My LT told me to see the medic and followed me to the clinic. The medic shined a light in my eyes. I blinked, felt spear tips jab through my temples. He told me I had a mild concussion. He asked me if I could still handle my AK, still walk, still drive.

I've forgotten a lot of things, but not the soldier's motto: I will always place the mission first, I will never accept defeat, I will never quit, and I will never leave a fallen comrade. Other guys had lost their arms and legs, I wasn't going to complain.

I told him yes.

That's good enough for me, the LT said.

I didn't know I was all screwed up. The next day I had a hard time concentrating. I understood just bits and pieces of conversations. Mouths moved but only a word or two stuck in my head. I rambled. Guys called me on it. What the fuck, man? You retarded or something? No, I said, I got a concussion, douchebag.

Weeks'd go by. A ringing in my ears kept me awake. Food lost its taste; the air, its odor of sand and wind. I'd see that kid and his mother near Tower Three and I'd scope them with my AK. Why do we let hajis so close to the walls? Why do we hire them to work on base? After what they did to me, three guys in my vic vaporized, why?

Then I started forgetting to Skype Katherine, forgot to email her too. When I did call, she told me I sounded stressed. What kind of a thing to say is that? I said. It's a war, you know. I didn't tell her what happened. I asked if she had sent my Christmas care package. It's only March, she said. Really? Bullshit. I thought she was fucking with me. That's not funny, I told her. I don't appreciate it.

When did you join the army?

Two thousand two.

Because of 9/11?

Yeah.

Two thousand two for me too, Jay says. Because of 9/11. It was like instinct. The thing to do. I thought I'd go to Afghanistan. Who were you with?

Fifteenth Brigade. Fort Sill.

Oklahoma?

Yeah.

That's where I'm from, Jay says. That wind down there throw off artillery shells during basic?

A little. Not dramatically.

I think I already asked you this. Have we had this conversation before?

I don't think so, I say.

I was hit by an IED several times, Jay says. One blew up eight feet from my face.

I got hit once by an IED. That was enough. Were you wearing arm guards and everything?

Yeah, that and more.

More? Fucking hot for more.

I was in a combat unit. I wanted to fight. You heard all the stuff going on and didn't want to miss it. I had two big machine guns. A .50 cal and an M249. My first time out, we were just passing a village. I was in the lead gun truck. The hajis started firing at us. I turned the turret to seven, eight o'clock and unloaded on them. It was night. I couldn't tell if I killed anybody. I felt like I had twenty cups of coffee.

I remember this one time, I tell Jay. Eastside at the gate. Sitting there, I had a .50 cal in the bunker. It was real quiet. Bunch of haji laborers waiting to come in. I heard a hiss right over our heads and then a whole wall blew to shit. Rocket or mortar, I don't know which. A loud hiss, then boom! That was my first time, first taste. Where were you at?

F.O.B Concord.

That's how I got all fucked up, I say. Going to Concord. Just outside Baghdad?

Yeah.

I look at Jay. Had I seen him in Iraq? I feel myself drifting, the memories crowding each other out. Jay's voice slows and fades to a whisper, like I'd turned down the volume. I understand what he's saying, but his words come to me in bits and pieces. I can no longer concentrate.

Maybe we have had this conversation before, I say.

One minute I'm in Iraq for nine months, the next I'm discharged and back home with Katherine and nothing in between. Our friends had this nonchalant attitude. They said, Hey, good to see you, what's up? as if I'd never left. The closeness I'd felt over there, the you're-in-Iraq, I'm-in-Iraq, we're-in-this-shit-together-bitches, that was gone. I plastered Operation Iraqi Freedom bumper stickers on the back of my car. I wanted people to know, but I didn't want to talk about it.

I couldn't sleep. I felt dark, depressed. At night, I lay on my back without moving so as not to disturb Katherine and stared at the ceiling without blinking until my eyes watered. She'd get up in the morning, but I'd stay in bed and think about Iraq. Like this one patrol. We go into a building, barely make it through the door when we see grenades dinking down the stairs. Six of our guys try to get out the door and bottleneck themselves up. I see a little bathroom and get in the stall. Tink, tink, tink, boom! Those six guys, they didn't make it.

Another time, funnier than shit, we were in Fallujah and an insurgent at the top of the stairs of this house shot an RPG and it hit the stair beneath Perez but nothing happened. It didn't go off. Perez yelled, I can't die! and charged up the stairs and blew that haji to shit. I laughed every time I thought of it, had to wipe tears away I was laughing so hard, and one morning Katherine heard me laughing, and she came into the bedroom and looked at me and started laughing too, like you do when you see someone laughing, and she wanted to know what's so funny. So I told her about Perez, how pissed he got when that fucking haji tried to waste him, I can't die! and how he sure the fuck did die on our way to F.O.B Concord, and she stopped laughing but I couldn't. She didn't get it. Then I stopped laughing. I wanted to grab and shake her, do you know what the real world is like? And then I started laughing again.

When I finished my alcohol program at the VA, I stuck pretty close to the house. I'd drop Katherine off at the supermarket and then drive away, forgetting about her. I took us to the movies, and when she asked me to buy her a Coke, I'd walk past the concession stand and wander outside and get lost in the parking lot and miss the movie. I'd go meet her for lunch at Buster's in North Beach, where she waitressed, but then I'd turn down the wrong street and drive to the Mission. I'd stop at a Mexican joint and call her and ask where the hell she was.

After I botched our fifth attempt at a lunch date, she ripped into me. This time I'd gone all the way to Oakland and called her from a pizza joint. A coworker gave her a lift to come get me. One look and I knew she was in no mood for pizza.

She drove us back home to the Richmond. We didn't say a word to each other. She pulled into the garage and I got out of the car and walked into the living room and turned on the TV. I wanted to be alone. Her anger crowded me, boxed me in. I saw things out of the corners of my eyes, turned and they vanished. I heard her throw her purse on the kitchen counter and knock over something and my shoulders jerked at the noise, and then she stood in front of me blocking the TV. I was eye-level to her waist. Her tan legs snaked out of this short summer dress. Her blouse rose up a bit and I could see her belly button. I didn't feel so crowded then. I reached for her. She pushed my hands away.

Are you seeing someone? she said. Is that why you're acting like this?

Hell no! I just forgot.

My heart started pounding like I was getting chewed by the LT for some dumb shit and my hands began shaking. She didn't get how I could forget something like lunch again and again, and I didn't either. I got it why she was so upset, but I didn't like her shouting at me.

Do you remember how we even met? You forget that?

I remembered. I had stopped for breakfast at Buster's a year before my enlistment. She took my order, two eggs easy, extra hash browns, two biscuits. We started talking. She had short, curly brown hair and a throaty voice I thought was kind of suggestive, and a smile that made me smile. I said we should see a movie. Maybe, she said.

It was love at first sight, I told her.

You're such a character, she said and blushed. Then she got shitty again. I think you're seeing someone.

Stop it, I said.

Don't tell me to stop it? Who is she?

Stop it!

Tell me her name!

I'd had it with her shouting. I smacked the end table with my first hard enough to make her jump and back away. I surprised myself, like a power surge had bolted up my ass without even a here-I-come. The word bullshit rolled around in my head like a marble getting louder and louder, faster and faster, and I pressed my hands against my forehead but I couldn't stop it, and

I screamed, Bullshit! Bullshit! Bullshit! and pounded the table again and again and the lamp fell and the bulb broke and I imagined all those pieces of glass rising in the air like shrapnel.

Katherine stood so still, eyes wide as plates, I thought she'd crack. I stared hard at her, balled my hands into fists, and laid a punch into the wall by the side of her head willing myself just in time not to put it through her face. I held my hand and stared at it like it didn't belong to me and ran into the garage. The air clung to me. I got in our car and spun out of the driveway, turned onto Lincoln Street and floored it for downtown with no idea what I'd do when I got there. I just wanted to go, get away, drive as fast as my heart was racing, but I hadn't gone far, hadn't even reached the Haight, when I rounded a curve and almost slammed into a line of stopped cars.

I stomped on the brakes and squealed to a stop, my heart a beating drum filling my head. What was the fucking holdup? I shifted into neutral, floored the accelerator to hear the engine whine, to hear noise, to hear it scream. I saw some flashing lights. I followed the car in front of me, riding its bumper with a desire to roll right over it, crushing it, and hear the metal break, beeping and pounding my hands on the steering wheel, keeping time to that marble still bouncing around inside my head, bullshitbullshitbullshitbullshit! A line of orange cones angled us into one lane and a cop waved us forward.

Sobriety checkpoint, he said. Keep moving.

I got sucked in, squeezed, cars on top of me front and back. One could explode at any moment. I cranked the radio. PSYOP would play Metallica to fuck with the hajis when we did house-to-house searches. Attention, attention, drop your weapons, someone would say through a bullhorn, and then they'd do this evil laugh. Then it was Metallica again on this big intercom thing. To keep the hajis from going to sleep and drive them crazy so they'd come out on their own and we could ripshit them to hell. I turned the radio louder until I couldn't turn the knob.

I watched the cop in my rearview mirror while another cop checked on the guy in front of me. Then it was my turn. He leaned into my open window and made a face at all the noise. He yelled at me to turn it down. I didn't touch it.

Having a good ol' time, rock star? he said.

Yes, sir, I said.

He asked where I had come from.

Nowhere, sir.

My heart was hammering my chest into splinters. I needed to keep moving. The AC didn't work. My window was down but sweat soaked my shirt. I opened the door to let more air in, my mouth dry as paste. The cop told me to close it.

Somewhere ahead of us I heard shouting. A squad car passed me on the shoulder of the road, stirring up small dust storms.

The cop shifted, moved his feet. I'm not going to tell you again.

More shouting up ahead and another squad car, going even faster, this one spitting stones from beneath its tires and hitting my car, tink, tink, tink. The dust exploded. Tink. I bolted from the car screaming and the cop grabbed me and we fell to the pavement and I clawed forward digging my fingers into the pavement. I knew what happened to prisoners. They got their heads cut off and shown on YouTube. I elbow-jabbed the cop and I heard him grunt. I rose to my knees and he knocked me flat with a punch to the back of the head and for a moment everything blazed white and then descended into deep black. He cuffed me. Another cop ran up and they both hauled me to my feet and the first cop shoved me against my car. I felt the hot metal burn my cheek, saw people leaning out their windows, the exhaust and wavering lines of heat making it look like their faces were under water.

Grenade? the cop holding me said.

I didn't say anything, listened to him breathing hard against me, my chest heaving. You were yelling "grenade."

I didn't say anything.

Your bumper stickers, Operation Iraqi Freedom. You a vet? he said.

I didn't say anything.

I was in Afghanistan, he said. Tenth Mountain Division, Khost Province.

I heard the rush of bodies running, descending on us. I felt them collecting in a huddle behind me, heard them blabbering haji mumbo jumbo. I tensed but the cop held me, his weight against me a kind of assurance. He told everyone to back off. He pressed me against the car for a long while, just the two of us breathing. Then he eased up and pulled me back. He gripped me by my right arm and stood beside me and we walked together to a squad car. I didn't try to run. I was not there, not anywhere. I watched myself from a great distance.

The cop opened the back door and put a hand on my head, guiding me inside. I liked the touch of his hand, the firm grip of his fingers in my hair. He closed the door. The AC blew cold air, covering me like clean sheets. When he got in, I asked him where we were.

I had a roadside bomb blow up eight feet from my face once, Jay said.

Remember when it was?

No. I was on foot patrol. Shook up my head too bad. I wish I did remember. People ask me stuff and I can't tell them. I can remember the kids I killed, but people don't want to hear about that. It's like saying I killed puppies. Three of them. I'm not proud of it, but I killed as many of them as I could.

It was them or you. Rule number one, Jay, come home alive.

We were getting supplies from one base back to our base. I forget which one. Not even a half hour out and we got ambushed. About seven, eight roadside bombs. The first one hit our truck and I blacked out for a couple seconds. I came to and pulled myself together. It was like Star Wars behind the truck. Firing on both sides, bombs going off, and our guys firing back. Jesus, it was loud. I spun the .50 cal in a circle toward the flashes of gunfire. When I got done firing, I looked at the side of the road. Four kids were connecting wires to set off the bombs. Ten, eleven, twelve years old, I don't know. I know I shot three of them. They kind of exploded from the .50 cal. The fourth ran away. I didn't get him.

What I remember of hajis dying I don't remember as good as Jay does. I see snapshots but details are missing. Like that kid and his mother near Tower Three. One day when I was returning sniper fire, I saw them take cover in a ditch. Then they were dead, blown to shit. Cut down just like that, and I didn't know what hit them. I want to say the sniper shot them but I don't know. Maybe it was me. I see them now bursting like popped water balloons. I think I'd remember if I shot them. But I don't. I don't remember. I just see them pop.

The cop took me straight to the VA. I don't know how long I stayed there, but it felt like hours. I had a CT scan and an MRI. A neuropsychologist asked me questions: Had I been injured in Iraq? When? Had I lost my ability to concentrate? He read something to me out of a magazine about a woman shopping. It wasn't long and I swear I listened but when he finished and asked me questions about what he had read, I had to admit I couldn't remember much. He kept on asking me stuff. I told him I needed a break.

Roger that, he said, and left.

Seconds later, the door opened and a shrink came at me: Did I get upset when I thought about Iraq? Did I get angry? Did the thoughts come out of nowhere? How did I react physically to those thoughts?

I don't remember what all else he asked me but it was a lot and I got pissed. Of course thinking about Iraq upset me, what kind of thing was that to ask? And how do I react physically? What does he think? I shit myself? But I kept myself in check. I didn't want to do another two-week stretch on the ninth floor.

When he finished, I sat by myself, exhausted and ready to sleep for days. I must've given someone my number and they called Katherine because she showed up out of nowhere to take me home. Before we left, the shrink and neuro guy compared notes in the hall. I watched them through a glass square in the exam room door. I closed my eyes, felt myself drifting, Katherine's hands on my shoulders. I heard the door open, heard their approaching footsteps. Then they stopped. I opened my eyes, looked at them standing above me. They said their preliminary diagnosis showed I had traumatic brain injury and post-traumatic stress disorder.

Preliminary diagnosis, shit. What did that mean? I didn't know and didn't care. I was beat-down, exhausted, and I didn't ask questions. They told Katherine I needed to make an appointment for more tests, more questions, their voices rolling in and out of my head like remote thunder. They gave her prescriptions to fill. I heard the paper crinkle in her hand and make a sharp sound as she folded it. She squeezed my shoulder when they said we could go.

Every morning in the weeks and months that followed, Katherine would remind me to take my anxiety, blood pressure, and headache pills. At night, she gave me a sleeping pill. Katherine was my rock, the left side of my brain. But when she asked for the divorce a year later she said it was because she couldn't rely on me anymore. She was never sure what I'd do. She understood it wasn't my fault, but still . . . The meds didn't seem to help my memory or calm my nerves. I saw a rehab counselor but Katherine didn't see me making much of a difference either. She felt alone. So she decided she might as well live alone. I told her I'd try harder, but I knew it was too late.

Yesterday I asked you to go to the Safeway and you drove to your mother's, she said, standing across from me in the kitchen. You sat on the swing set in the backyard and she had to persuade you to come home.

I didn't remember. Maybe I just needed to be alone. The distant roar of an oncoming headache came on full bore up the back of my neck, getting louder and louder. I reached over the pile of dirty plates, pots, and pans in the sink and shut the blinds to block the sun. I closed my eyes because of the headache. I turned the faucet on and began washing plates as fast as I could, water splashing onto the counter and me, thinking that would make her happy. She stepped beside me, dried the plates I'd cleaned, and put them away. She put a hand out to slow me down. She turned off the water. Neither of us spoke. We had Post-its on the cabinet doors with reminders about what goes where so I could have shelved them myself, but she was done giving me chances.

A sparrow lands on the picnic table and hops toward the wafers. Jay reaches out with a finger and tries to stroke its head but it flies away. I catch the plastic bag before it blows off the table.

I can't believe we ate all this shit, I say.

Yeah, Jay says. Have to see a dentist, I guess.

Go in and say, Here we are, doc.

Here we are, Jay says.

He smiles. I don't expect a laugh and he doesn't give me one. I get up, take the torn cellophane wrappers, put them in the bag and toss them into a trash can. I'm tired, wrung out. It's time to go home. I've got Katherine's number if I get lost, if I remember to look for it to call her. She let me keep the house. That was good of her. Finding a new place and dealing with the unfamiliarity of it, well, I'm glad I didn't have to do that. Yes, I am. Katherine's a good person, I know that. She got tired. I get it. I try to. I can't forget her. I'm not saying I want to necessarily, but given I've forgotten so much else, why not her? It's a little unfair, I think.

I slap crumbs off my hands, watch some guys cutting the grass. They kneel, pull weeds, stand, and clip dead branches off bushes. Everybody I know works. That's how a guy defines himself.

What do you do? people ask.

I'm a disabled vet, I say.

I walk back to Jay. He stares at me with a look that says he's not seeing me or anybody else. I notice some doctors standing around in a group. I guess they're doctors. I hope one of them's a shrink and sees Jay. I wonder what they're saying. Sometimes I overhear people talking about the war. Should've done this, they say. Should've done that. Had I been in charge this, this, and this would have happened.

Had I been in charge, shit. Let them talk. It's a free country. Everyone's entitled to an opinion. If they were to ask for mine, I'd say life is full of surprises. Then I'd walk away and leave them to whatever surprises might await.

Walter

I wake up with the shakes, my throat dry as sandpaper, my tongue pasty tasting. Kicking out of my sleeping bag all kinds of jittery, I reach for my plastic jug with one hand, uncap it, and tip it over my other hand. Water spills onto my palm. I splash my face and rub my beard, flicking drops into the air. Drag my hand across my T-shirt to dry it. Then I drink, gripping the jug in both trembling hands. Swallow. Fill my mouth again, gargle, and spit. I drink some more, the shakes extending into my arms. I spill water down my chest. My blue pants feel like weights on my legs.

A few suits on Clay Street walk past my alley. Well, not mine. The police remind me of that at least once a week when they tell me to move. Last month, they said I could stay but I couldn't keep my tent. They put on plastic gloves, broke it down, and threw it in the back of a pickup. I got to keep my blanket and sleeping bag. That's enough, I guess. I put the blanket inside the sleeping bag and some cardboard beneath the bag so I don't get chilled from the pavement. It gives me a little cushion but not much. I'm pretty stiff when I wake up.

I roll my neck, hear the joints make cracking sounds. Squeezing my arms against my sides, I feel a chill run through me. The suits don't spare me a glance. I hear cell phones ring, voices raised but not clear enough for me to understand what they're saying. I make out only a few words. Some of the suits pause to look up as if they worry it might rain but only a thinning layer of fog lingers above all of us. We share the weather. We have that much in common. I watch pigeons flutter to get out of the way of guys from other camps maneuvering shopping carts loaded with blankets around the suits. They too don't look my way. I know some of them, but I won't share my site with them. They'll want what I have. I don't know what they'll take when I nod out.

Twisting the cap back on my jug, I stash it, my sleeping bag, blanket, and a baggie with a spoon and a can opener beneath a dumpster across the alley from the back door of an Italian restaurant. One of the cooks comes out with an aluminum-wrapped sandwich and offers it to me. His schedule changes every week. I never know when he'll be on, but when he is he always when gives me food. I unwrap the aluminum. A meatball sandwich. Probably left over from yesterday. A little hard on the stomach this early in the morning, especially the way I'm feeling. I can't imagine eating it. The thought turns my stomach. I need a bottle. I wrap it back up.

I shouldn't do this. You need to stop expecting handouts, the cook tells me, the same thing he always says each time he gives me food. I don't know where he gets off with that. I've never once asked him for anything.

He hurries back inside. The hinges of the door creak and the lock clicks behind him. I put the sandwich in my shoulder bag and clean my little area, throw two empty Thunderbird bottles and a tuna fish can into the dumpsters, the noise a stick up my ass jolting my fucking nerves. Got to keep my camp right or the restaurant might call the police, but shit, man, shit, that noise, God damn, it got my heart banging. I hold my head in my hands. I feel bloated, woozy, and still thirsty. My body's telling me what it needs, wine, but I have no money. I sit down, put my head between my knees. The shakes jolt through me and I grip my knees. Maybe I drank more than two bottles. I don't think so. I close my eyes. A wind blows. I feel the dampness of my shirt against my skin.

Footsteps. The sound of someone walking toward me. I don't look up. They stop. I feel them near me. I feel them looking down at me. I wait but they don't speak. Maybe they think I'm passed out. I wait to be nudged, told to move. If it's the cops, they might put me in a paddy wagon this time, take me to the Bryant Street station or drop me off at Fresh Start. I'd get in a detox program there. At Bryant, I'd probably be held for the day in the drunk tank.

I wait. Nothing. Finally, I raise my head and open my eyes to a woman staring down into my face. She has on sunglasses and I can't see her eyes. A yellow sweater hangs off her shoulders, puffing up with a breeze that stirs the trash and plastic bags ensnared on a wire fence behind the dumpster. She wears dark slacks with sharp creases and heels. We both cover our faces until the wind stops and the dust settles. Maybe this woman's an outreach worker for some agency and is handing out food and bottles of water. She's dressed pretty nice for that.

Excuse me, she says. I've just been going around to people I see, you know, people like you, and I saw you here, and I wanted to ask if, well, have you, I mean, have you seen this man?

She removes a paper from her purse and gives it to me. I look at her pale fingers, nails polished red, and reach for it, embarrassed by my quivering hands. I hold it against my knees and read: *Missing. Brian Hanson. Five feet, ten inches tall. Twenty-eight years old. Last seen on Haight and Masonic.* A photo of a young man stares out at me from below the words. He has blond hair and a lean face. The veins in his neck show. A thin smile, dull brown eyes.

Do you recognize him? she asks me.

111

No, I say. The first word of the day. It croaks out of my mouth. I clear my throat, want to spit but not in front of her. Swallow instead, a slimy wafer, and I cough and end up spitting it out anyway. She doesn't react, doesn't move. Taking off her glasses, the woman pinches the top of her nose like she has a headache. I don't tell her but I think she looks like this Brian Hanson a little bit.

Sorry, I say. Is he on the street?

How does this happen? she asks.

A group of pigeons rise, wings flapping noisily, and they soar above us, blinkering the pale sunlight. The restaurant door opens. A woman in a red-stained apron leans out and heaves a trash bag. It arcs through the air and falls with a clatter of breaking glass into the dumpster. She notices me and then the woman and hesitates before she turns and shuts the door.

I don't know. It just does, I tell her.

I look at the paper again as if somehow a second look will help me recognize this guy. I don't. I wish I didn't feel so on-the-spot. I wish I didn't have the shakes. I wish I had some wine. I can't move. Shaking too bad.

Are you all right? she asks me.

I nod. I must look like I'm vibrating to pieces. Feels like it.

I don't know him, I say.

I've been handing out his picture to people, you know, to people in, well, your situation. What I imagine is your situation. Like you, they haven't seen him.

Still staring at the paper, I think of how sometimes, at Fresh Start, I ask one of the social workers if I can use a computer to look up a job. I don't think anyone believes me but they set me up. I get on and go to Facebook and find people I knew long ago, like in high school, but none of their pictures match my memory of them. Of course they're older, I get that, but still . . . I've even looked up my mother, Susan Johns. Not my mother, her name.

She died from a stroke because of high blood pressure, probably from drinking, so I can't look her up for real. Instead, I check out other women with the same name. There're a lot of Susan Johnses. None of them look like her and many are younger than she would be now if she were alive, but it's like she's not gone when I see her name, and I read what a particular Susan Johns posted, as if she was my mother. It's something to do when I get to feeling a certain way, but their posts don't make any sense. They talk about people I don't know. One Susan Johns said she was going to the Grand Canyon next month. My mother would have had no interest in the Grand Canyon. Deserts weren't her thing.

You can call me if you see him, the woman says.

She points to the bottom of the page at a phone number.

You probably don't have a phone, do you? Maybe you know somebody who does?

Fresh Start lets me use their phones, I say.

Sometimes, I find a magazine with a subscription insert. I call the 800 number on it and when someone answers, I pretend I'm interested in subscribing. I'll go, How much a month does it cost? How often will I get the magazine? How long is the subscription? I try to loosen them up and get them talking. Where's your office? I'll ask. What's the weather like where you are? Are you having a busy day? Sometimes they sound like they're from another country. I spoke to one guy who was in India. I asked him what it was like there and he got to talking all about Mumbai. You should visit, he said. Oh, I will, I said. I plan to. On my next vacation. After a while, he got back to business and asked me for my credit card number. I apologized, told him I didn't have it with me but that I'd call him right back. You won't get me, you'll get somebody else. That's OK, I said. I didn't call back. He didn't expect me to, I think. Maybe he knew. I don't know. I just wanted to talk.

I look at this Brian guy's photo again. If he's a drinker I might run into him. Drugs, no. I don't hang with tweakers. I know one guy, he's a drinker now, but back in the day he used heroin. He got on methadone to kick it. He tells me he doesn't understand why younger people use meth. Crazy shit, he said. Back in his day, it was just smack. We're old, Walter, he tells me. A different generation, you and me.

I checked with the police, but he's not there, she says.

She looks past me, her eyes tearing up. I turn away. She takes a Kleenex from her purse and dabs her nose. Then she points at his name on the paper as if I haven't noticed it and presses the Kleenex against her nose again.

His name is Brian Hanson. This isn't anything any of us ever expected.

Have you tried the homeless shelters?

Yes.

Traffic picks up on Clay. Buses stop two deep, letting people off. Cars beep, and more and more people hurry along the sidewalk. Long shadows creep up the sides of buildings. I should get up, I think. Go to the detox at Fresh Start. These shakes. Fuck that. I need a bottle.

Thank you, she says again.

She offers me five dollars. I look at it. There's my morning wine. The bill flutters between us. I feel better, my heart not hammering my chest so hard. I've been delivered.

Call that number if you see him, even if you're not sure it's him, she says.

I will, I say.

Take care.

I take the five. She turns around and walks toward Clay. Pausing, she looks back at me.

Call.

I watch her leave, hear the sharp click of her shoes on the pavement. At the end of the alley, she turns right and disappears. I rest my head between my knees and close my eyes. In a minute, I'll walk around to the drop-in center at Fresh Start and ask guys, You seen this dude? Do you recognize him? I'll call her and say, I've not found him but I'm working on it. Or I got a lead, someone who looks just like him. Maybe we'll meet somewhere and go over what I've pieced together. Maybe. Maybe not. Not. I'll get a bottle is what I'll do. Need to do.

Wrapping my arms around my knees a little harder, I rock back and forth, back and forth, trying to summon the control to stop shaking long enough to stand and make it to a liquor store. The flier drifts from my fingers and falls by my feet, gets picked up by a breeze. I shiver, watch it dance in the air, bobbing and weaving like nothing else matters, Brian's face hovering above me until it gets plastered to the fence with other garbage.

Carol

I've been drinking for most of the day today, and I don't know why but I started thinking about Jason. Memories creep up on me when I get full, I guess. Besides, it's only been two days since I found him dead in the hall. Jason lived in the room next to mine at the McLeod Hotel. He was a one-man show and I enjoyed being his audience. He made me laugh. If I wasn't around, he talked up our other neighbor, another one of us drunks named Walter. Sometimes, I'd hear him shout, His name is Walter, and he's a helluva guy! And I'm embarrassed to say I'd feel a little jealous, like I'd worry he'd start spending all his time with Walter and not me. Jason took up space is what I'm saying. In a good way. When he wasn't around, I felt the silence. A new guy I don't know lives in his room now.

I told Katie at Fresh Start about Jason. She said she was sorry but she didn't know him. How sorry can she be? Maybe she was sorry for me because he was my friend, but she didn't know that. She might have assumed it or why else would I have told her? She said, Sorry, like most people say, Good morning. You say it just to say it. Anyway, I'm happy for her. Katie and I used to run the streets together before she got sober. I miss her. It's hard to hang out with someone you used to drink with who has stopped drinking. Sort of like a rich bitch spending time with a poor gal. So I don't see her much unless she's working when I'm in detox. There's too much that separates us now. But I can't get mad at her. She has this kind face, pebbled with pale freckles as if she's still a kid. How do I get angry with someone who looks like that? Her street name was Sunshine. Everyone just called me Carol. Sunshine and Carol. Katie's one of those people who can smile and look sad at the same time. You're going to die, Carol, she told me the last time I was in detox. She's right, and after I'm gone, she'll still be alive—another thing that will separate us. I've offered her a drink more than a few times when I've seen her walking to work but she won't have it. I'm always glad she turns me down but a little jealous too. I know she doesn't think she's better than me, but sometimes it feels that way. She's given up on me, I know, but we were partners at one time, I remind myself, the best of friends. Still are but aren't. It feels weird for her to tell me I'm going to die, like I'm terminal with cancer or something. In a way, I suppose I am. Terminal, I mean. I'm not going to stop drinking, so that's terminal. Good for Katie to quit but not for me. I think about it but it scares me. To wake up one morning knowing this is it. Life is going to come at me and I won't be high or nothing. That I'll just have to deal with it. That's frightening, for real. On the bright side, if I die like she says I will, I won't disappoint. I can die. I can do that much right.

I might go to detox tonight to have some company. I got pretty used to Jason and now he's left me. He moved in about a month after I did. He took the room that a guy named Lyle had. I didn't know Lyle but Katie did. Said the three of us had drunk together, but I don't remember him. Two days before Jason showed up, the manager found Lyle dead on his bed, arms spread like Jesus on the cross, a mickey of Thunderbird in one hand, sheets stained red with spilled wine. The manager left Lyle's door open when he ran to his office to call the paramedics and I looked in. Lyle's eyes were open, staring, the expression on his face like someone who had just remembered something he wanted to say and died before he could get it out. Now that would be frustrating. He wasn't wearing a shirt or pants, just a pair of drawers. His bare feet hovered above the floor. Maybe he was getting ready for bed. The glow from the ceiling light haloed his bald head. A jacket and a pair of jeans hung off the back of a chair. Beneath the chair, dark socks and a pair of sneakers. Two rats on the windowsill rose on their feet like curious neighbors peering through the glass. The paramedics came, covered him with a sheet, and wheeled him out on a gurney. A couple of days later, Jason moved in.

I was coming out of my room one morning when I met him for the first time. Everyone calls me Tenderloin Jason, he told me, or sometimes Louisiana Jason because I hail from Baton Rouge. Shit, I've been here for years, know everyone, so I'm more Tenderloin than Louisiana now.

He pronounced every sound of every letter of every word he spoke. Even when he said, Shit, he came down hard on the "t" like a pencil snapping, the rhythm of his Southern accent rolling that snap into the next word like dominoes. I do not hold conversations, he told me. I declaim.

He told me how he stopped at Fred's Liquor on Sixth most mornings and then at Walgreens to pick up blood pressure meds from the pharmacy, how he would then wander home past St. Anthony's soup kitchen, sometimes stopping at the Comeback Club, until he returned to the McLeod and to his room to imbibe, as he put it. He stopped talking only long enough to raise a bottle of peach schnapps to his mouth. When he drained the last drop, he would point in my direction and sing out, Her name is Carol, and she's a helluva gal! and I'd blush. Not too many people can make me blush, but he could, and it felt kind of good to feel that rush of red to my face, tingling and hot.

Jason dressed pretty snazzy. He liked to wear gray pants and white button-down shirts he collected from Salvation Army thrift stores. On the first of the month, he used some of what was left of his general assistance check to have his clothes pressed at a Guerrero Street dry cleaner. He showered and shaved every day and combed his hair. Like he had a job in the financial district or something. I have to say, he kind of inspired me. I started bathing more or less regularly, sometimes in the bathroom down the hall but mostly I used the sink in my room, and every other morning before I started drinking I'd make it a point to get a change of clothes at Fresh Start. Even tidied up my room by putting my bottles in the wastebasket before I passed out so I wouldn't wake up to a mess on the floor.

One night, Jason took out his phone and showed me black-and-white photos of a studio apartment he had rented decades ago: a sleeper sofa against one wall, a circular rug, a desk, and a rack of suits in a closet. He pointed out a photograph of himself on the wall behind the sofa. In the picture, he was wearing a suit and tie. His brown hair, combed up from his forehead, stood out against the gray wall, and he had a smile, the kind of smile that creases your face and you feel confident as hell. It was sort of a posed, swept-back kind of look that made me think of Hollywood celebrity photos from back in the day, like in the 1930s or '40s or something. He was twenty-five then, he said. I could hear in his voice, the soft way he spoke, how long ago that was. He taught ballroom dancing on cruise ships. Bullshit, I said. Au contraire, Carol, he scolded. Standing, a little wobbly from drinking, he began moving across my room, dipping and turning, arms out like he was holding a partner. When he stopped, I clapped. I half-hoped he'd ask me to dance, but he just stared at me and then kind of slowly he gave me one of Katie's sad smiles and bowed. He looked almost the same as he did in that old photo. His stomach protruded like a bowling ball but his gray hair remained just as thick, his face almost free of wrinkles. That's pretty good for a drinker. My hair is as gray as an overcast sky and I got bags under my eyes the size of hammocks. But I wasn't as sad as Walter. I wasn't trying to hide my looks. He wore a black toupee that sat on his head like a helmet. White bits of hair stuck out around his ears, and sometimes he'd swagger in, boozed up, and looking all smug because he had a beat-down ten-dollar crack whore with him. That toupee made me laugh, but not Jason. He didn't make fun of Walter or any of the other people here, at least not with me. He'd just go and talk about himself like he was the only one that mattered. Maybe by taking up so much oxygen he figured no one would have enough air to say anything bad about him. He told me he used to work at a furniture warehouse in Oakland with a gal named Jerry. The ballroom dancing stuff had been a summer job, a young man's job. Rich, middle aged ladies wanted pretty young things. We only stay pretty so long, Carol, Jason told me. The warehouse wasn't bad. Lifting sofas and tables kept him in shape, even if it didn't keep him pretty. I thought of Jason hefting furniture. I thought of him lifting me in his arms on the dance floor like I was nothing. That feeling of holding someone and of being held and I was lost for a moment. Then Jason brought me back by asking if I had a towel. I gave him one. He wiped sweat from his forehead and took deep breaths. I offered him my bottle of T-bird. He shook his head. Not my vintage, Carol, he said. He reached into his back pocket for his blood pressure meds. He popped two tablets into his mouth and took a deep swallow from his schnapps bottle.

Jason and I could stay sober for two or three days when we wanted. It was easier on warm days. With the sun out, I didn't feel so desolate. We'd watch TV in the lobby. Bored, sure, but not depressed. Well, maybe a little. We'd look through the windows and watch all the people on the sidewalk and think we had plenty of time to go outside and enjoy the sun, and then before we knew it, it was dark and we were still in the lobby and that was that. Jason, I said one night, we waste a lot of time drinking. Maybe we should do something like try a program again. But which one would take us? he'd say. And what agency would refer us that hadn't before? It got kind of overwhelming thinking about it and we started drinking again because of all our options that was the one sure thing.

On cold days when the air could get kind of weepy with fog, we drank without thinking we'd do something else. My mom drank on cloudy days. Sunny days too, but she'd start early if it was overcast. If it was nice out, she'd hold off until night and rush around the house trying to keep occupied by cleaning windows or vacuuming. I get it now. Her nerves were shot, and she couldn't sit still. She and my dad had divorced when I was so little that I can't remember him; he didn't come around, and mom cleaned houses but she didn't get work every day. On her off days, she'd go out to get coffee and then run out again to buy bread whether we needed it or not, and then she'd go out and get something else. She was wound up from not drinking. I stayed away from her until about midday when she seemed to adjust to not having any booze. She slowed down, napped. At night, she'd hold off until after we ate dinner, pizza or something, and then she'd ask me for a glass of sherry. I was a kid, not even a teenager, and I'd sit next to her and do my homework until she got drunk enough she let me have a glass. I had no tolerance then. I'd be out after a couple of swallows, my head on her lap.

The sun was shining when Jason died like fifteen, maybe thirty minutes after he'd stopped to sit down with me in the hotel lobby. I was pretty-well lit from drinking that morning. He had walked in holding a Walgreens bag, took a chair, and talked about the kind of food he once ate on Easter. That was Jason. He'd just come up with these thoughts like from nowhere. He sipped from his bottle making a face with each swallow. Not going down with its natural flow, today, he said. Then Walter came around and got played by a prostitute. I nodded off in my chair and didn't hear Jason leave. I don't know how long I was out. When I woke up my mouth tasted like paste. I stood and went to my room, my whole body shaking. I was out of Thunderbird and I thought I'd have to hit up Jason for some of his schnapps. Too sweet for me, but all I needed was one swallow to get right enough to walk to the liquor store. When I reached my floor, the hall seemed really long and the light seemed kind of weak and I saw Jason on his side on the floor outside his room. I moved slow. I knew something bad had happened, but I was just in a fog and stuck in first gear. I touched his shoulders, noticed his schnapps bottle poking out of his pocket. His chest wasn't moving. My heart started racing, clearing my head. Call 911, I began yelling to no one, Call 911. But I knew it was too late. Walter stumbled out of his room all herky-jerky. He had probably been passed out. He looked at me, trying to understand what was happening. What's wrong? What's wrong? he said again and again, as other doors opened down the hall. I grabbed Jason's schnapps before Walter got any ideas and put it in my pocket. I wanted to call Katie. It was after six. She wouldn't be at work. By the time I'd get around to seeing her, she'd know and it wouldn't matter. Jason wasn't her client.

This sucks, Jason, I said.

Someone must have called the police because they showed up with two paramedics. One of the paramedics carried a red box that resembled a tool kit. I told them what I knew, which wasn't anything. The police told me to move. The paramedics examined Jason. He's gone, one of them said. They put him on a gurney and covered him just like they'd done with Lyle. I stared at the outline of Jason's body. It occurred to me I didn't know his last name.

The paramedics left. They never did open that red box. The hall emptied, snap, just like that, as if Jason had never been there. I mean I stared at the floor where he had collapsed but I didn't even see a spot, an impression on the carpet, nothing. I went to my room and sat on the edge of my bed. This is my life, I thought. It was one thing to be told I was drinking myself to death. It was another thing to see someone who did. He was gone, like really gone. I unscrewed the cap of the schnapps and took a swallow. Too sweet, really, but I could get used to it. It gave me a buzz, for sure, chilled my nerves. Late afternoon light shone through the windows. I wanted to cry. Or, I guess, I thought I should cry but nothing came. He was so gone. I wondered if I'd even really known him. Of course I had, but it was just me now, no Jason, and I had questions like: Where were you born? Where'd you grow up? Little things like that. Just who the fuck are you, Jason? I went through my empty T-bird bottles and shook them over a glass to see what dregs I could get after I finished the schnapps. I got some. I sat back on my bed and thought of Jason. I imagined him beside me drinking. I could feel him squeeze my right hand, lean close to my face and say in that way he liked to talk, Au revoir mon cher amour, and then in my mind I watched him go to his room. Fuck him, he could make me blush! In the morning, suffering, as he liked to say, from the turbulence of a frightful hangover—where did he come up with this way of talking?—he would get up and make his schnapps run. He'd come back, face all red from walking and tell me about how the streets were jammed with people doing the buying and selling of, Well, Carol, we are not talking Girl Scout cookies. We mean crack cocaine and heroin and any prescription drug you can name.

I sat with his schnapps bottle and could just see him doing the weave and duck on McAllister Street until I felt myself becoming him, swaying on my bed like I'm Jason walking. Excuse me, excuse me, watch out sweethearts, I said in that voice of his. Excuse me, excuse me, and Carol, I saw the police cruisers coasting their slow crawl, checking out people—who all of a sudden walked away, I'm cool officer, I'm cool—looking for a dealer, an informant, someone in the middle of a score, whoever the cops could find to make their quota of arrests for that day, and I saw a young man, short hair, blue jeans, T-shirt, fake leather jacket, rolling up his sleeve in front of this other guy. He wasn't showing off his latest tattoo, no, he was showing the dealer his track marks, his need. The dealer saw the black lines, waited for the cops to pass out of sight, and then relaxed and waved the guy, a kid really, forward, digging into a shirt pocket for a baggy of the white stuff, and I kept going, downhill on Leavenworth and across Civic Center Plaza to Fred's.

Standing in front of a shelf of bottles, I drummed my fingers against my legs until I found peach schnapps and took two bottles.

Here you go, Larry, I said to the man behind the counter.

Ahh, Jason, he said. How are you?

Fragile as glass, Larry, but I'll make it.

He put each bottle in a bag and twisted the tops. I paid him.

His name is Larry, and he's a helluva guy.

See you, Jason.

Larry reminded me of Jerry, my supervisor at a furniture warehouse in Oakland. He'd always say "job site." I got to go to the Richmond job site, he'd say, I got to go to the Concord job site. When we got off work, he said, Are you going to drink tonight? and before I could answer, he'd go, I was going to stop by a bar and have one. I'd go with him and we always had more than one, but that was the routine. We worked mornings, six to two, then my schedule changed to the swing shift. That gave me too much time to kill before work and I'd have one or two or three in the morning and after a while, you know, I lost count and I started clocking in late until I just stopped clocking in. Things would have been different if I'd kept my morning hours.

At the corner of Sixth and Market, I turned into Walgreens to pick up my blood pressure meds. As I waited for the pharmacist to ring them up, I noticed a basket of chocolate rabbits displayed on the shelf.

Is it almost Easter? I asked.

Yes, she said. Almost, like tomorrow.

She dropped two bottles in a bag and handed it to me. I looked at her name tag.

Her name is Michelle, and she's a helluva gal.

She smiled, shaking her head.

I followed Post Street uphill to Ellis, past St. Anthony's and the line of men and women waiting for the cafeteria to open. The sidewalk, grimed black from trash and spilled food, pulled at the bottom of my shoes. I felt hot as if I'd been running and I took off my jacket and opened one of the schnapps bottles. Pigeons hopped out of my way and I passed a barefoot man, his jacket spattered with bird shit, who talked to himself in a harsh, fevered whisper, spitting out words between the gaps of his yellowed teeth. He warned away invisible tormentors. I walked two more blocks before I reached Ellis, stepping around a man hosing down the sidewalk outside a convenience store. Hookers trolled the sidewalk, clomping stiff-legged in their square, black platform shoes.

When I reached the McLeod, I saw you, Carol, half-asleep, in the lobby and I sat down. Her name is Carol, and she's a helluva gal! but you did not wake up until I shook you. I asked you if you thought it was hot out and you said, No. I drank from my bottle but I felt bloated. I unscrewed the caps of my blood pressure meds, took two tablets. Carol, I said, I saw a chocolate bunny at Walgreens. It's Easter tomorrow. Do you remember Easter? My mother made ham. What did your family have? I had to shake you again and repeat myself. You said, What? I repeated myself before you told me your mother made ham too. Turkey on Christmas, ham on Easter.

Yes, I agreed. We should get some ham tomorrow.

OK, you said. Where would we cook it?

Good point, I said. No ham for tomorrow.

There's always St. Anthony's.

There is that, I agreed.

The door opened and I raised my arms against the light until it closed. Carol, wouldn't you know it was Walter sauntering in with one of the hookers I'd just seen. He stopped and fingered through an ashtray for a smoke. All class, our Walter. The prostitute stood stiffly beside him. Circles of pink rouge made her pale, tense face appear even paler. Walter winked at me and started walking upstairs. She followed him. Where's my money? she said. I got it, he said. I want to see your money first, she said, her voice pushing him. I got it, he snapped. I looked at you, Carol, and rolled my eyes, and you shook your head. I took another swallow of schnapps. I heard someone running down the stairs and Walter yelled, Hey! and the prostitute rushed by us out the door, and Walter stumbled after her a few feet behind. After a moment, he walked back in, out of breath.

She took my money, he said.

His fly was open, unseemly to say the least. He stared at the floor as if it was speaking to him. He looked more hopeless than angry. A car horn blared outside. The hotel doors opened, pushed by the wind. Walter chewed on his lower lip. He turned to me like he was about to say something, but I looked away.

He kicked the ashtray. It wobbled but did not fall. He walked upstairs. A sense of embarrassment for him spread through me, and I resented him for imposing on me in that way. I had experienced enough of my own humiliations. I did not need to share his. I looked at you, Carol, but your eyes were half-closed. She's Carol, and she's a helluva gal! But you did not wake up and this time I did not shake you. I stood and felt sick to my stomach. I sat back down. My left arm tingled. Standing again I gripped the banister and began walking up the stairs shaking my arm to get rid of the prickly sensation. When I reached my room, I felt an incredible pain in my chest that webbed out and up into my throat and I gasped and before I had time to find my keys, before I understood I would be leaving you alone for this night and all the other nights to follow, before you even entered my mind, Carol, I was gone.

Katie

I clock in.

Hey, good looking, Hank says.

He's always hitting on me. He's not handsy about it, just kind of flirty. Sometimes he'll bump against me, but I don't mind. I like him but not in that way. He knows. As long as he does, and he doesn't get handsy, I'm OK with it.

He hands me a clipboard with a list of detox clients. It's the first of the month. Everyone got their checks so most of our beds are empty. Beds. They're actually exercise mats on the floor with a blanket and a sheet and a pillow. We had beds once, but clients pissed themselves and ruined the mattresses. So now we have mats.

Hank points out a guy on mat two. No name. A John Doe. Just came in, Hank says. Too drunk to do an intake. He doesn't know him. Thought maybe I would. I take a look. Young. A pale red plaid shirt covers his thin chest. Strings of blond hair stick to his forehead. I don't recognize him.

Hank wrote, "10:30 p.m.," by the guy's name, the time he checked him in. I start at eleven. I wonder if the guy had really been that drunk or if Hank just didn't want to do the intake because it was so close to quitting time. Put him on a mat, leave the paperwork for me. He may dig on me but that don't mean he's not lazy. I give Hank a look

Don't do me like that, Katie, he says. It ain't about that. He was too drunk.

He goes on: One of our regulars, Walter Johns, asked for detox and told Hank that there was a man passed out on the sidewalk in front of Fresh Start. Walter didn't know him. Hank did Walter's intake and then went outside with a volunteer. The guy was laying on his back by a trash bin. Hank shouted at him and he kind of mumbled and rolled onto his side. Hank and the volunteer put on plastic gloves and lifted him up under the arms and half-carried, half-walked him inside. They put him on a mat to sleep it off.

Go over and look at him, Hank says. Maybe you know him.

I will. Can I have some coffee first?

Hank's the super on the swing shift; I'm working the overnight shift. I'm in charge tonight because my super called in sick, so it's just me and another guy, Joe, working. He's what our boss, Tom, calls a paid intern. He's a graduate student at the School of Social Work at San Francisco State University. In staff meetings, Tom talks about how we should all follow Joe's example and go to school, get a college degree. I don't know what Tom's thinking. He's not an alcoholic, that's one thing. He started here years ago doing community service to work off parking tickets and got hired. He went back to school, graduated college. I was still a client then, but I remember staff complaining how Tom was getting promoted ahead of them because he had a degree and they didn't. He's nice enough but he doesn't know. Neither does Joe, and he's nice enough too. Real eye candy. Got an ass that won't quit. I'm just saying. But he didn't drink half his life away like the rest of us. AA meetings are our classes. Our sobriety chips are our degrees. Tom thinks it's too easy to go from the street to work at the place where we detoxed. He likes to think that's what he did, but he didn't. He had a job delivering pizzas and he got another job working with drunks, that's what he did. Good for him. He went to school. Not all of us will. Not all of us want to risk failing. That's one good way to start drinking again. We got no work history to get hired anywhere else but Fresh Start. We know the clients. We used to drink with them. That's a kind of education. Tom should be satisfied with that. If he's so big on college, hire those kinds of people. He can't because the pay is too low. But we'll take it. Aim higher, he says. If you're drowning you can't just be satisfied with a life preserver. You got to swim toward shore. He doesn't know. The life preserver is my sobriety. I hang on to it a day at a time like the Big Book says.

Hank clocks out, lights a smoke, and sits at a table in detox. Before he got sober five years ago, he was beaten up one night and woke up in San Francisco General unable to see because his eyes were all swole up. That was it. That did it. Not being able to see freaked him out and he got into a recovery program and stopped drinking. He smokes too much. His sandpaper voice deep with hard scratches. Cigarettes will kill you just like alcohol, but I figure you can only give up so many addictions in one lifetime. He's quit enough shit. He's also losing his hearing in his left ear. Whoever beat him up gave that side of his head a good workout. When I talk to him, he cups his bad ear with his left hand, and he leans into me like something unseen is pushing him. He did my last intake. I don't know if I can do this, I told him. You'll be OK, he said in that voice of his. I know, I said, a day at a time. I've heard it all before. You haven't heard this, he said. At first you got to take it a minute at a time. Tell yourself, I won't drink for sixty seconds. Then take it to the next sixty.

I followed his advice. He wasn't hitting on me then. He was like a big brother. Still is. He just gets flirty. A minute at a time became a day at a time. Some days are harder than others. Some days, I'm back to a minute at a time. Little things. Like a cloudy day, something that simple and my mind goes dark. I get depressed. Sixty seconds, Katie, I go, sixty seconds. You'd think after almost two years sober I'd have it down, but the urge to drink is like an allergy. You never know what's going to set you off sneezing. It's a big deal to Hank that he did my last intake. That I stopped drinking after he put me in detox. Like he had a hand in it, and he did, but I'm the one who chose to stop. He didn't make that choice. He didn't stop me from buying a bottle. I stopped me. That's my ego talking, I know. Ego can lead to anger and anger can lead to drinking. I should be grateful to Hank. I am. I just wish I liked him the way he's liking on me. Being alone, that can be hard too. Sixty seconds, Katie. Count. Sixty seconds.

Walter stirs from his mat. He sits staring at his feet. Getting up, walking stiff-legged, he staggers as if the floor has slanted to one side. He moves toward Hank, his right arm stretched out to grab the back of a chair. He sits. Hank gets him a cup of coffee and Walter tries to drink it but his hands shake. He sets the cup on the table, leans forward, and sips. His lined face drains into his chin like it might slide right off. He and Hank ran together on the street when Hank was still drinking. Everyone he knows is on the street. I may have drunk with Walter too, when I was out there, I don't remember. Probably. I drank from, like, when I was fourteen to must've been thirty-four, thirty-five, maybe. I watch Hank and Walter talking. It's quiet, I might join them. Everyone I know is either still drinking or in recovery. How do you see someone outside that loop? I wonder. What would Joe and I talk about?

I'll do the bed check, Joe says.

OK, I say, and give him the clipboard.

Every half hour we walk through detox to make sure the clients are OK. By OK, I mean breathing. Used to be we checked on them once an hour, but last year a client, Carol, died in detox so now we check on them every thirty minutes. I'm not sure it matters. If someone stops breathing five minutes after we check on them, what are we supposed to do? I guess we'd do our walk-throughs every fifteen minutes. Pretty soon we'll be sitting beside them until they wake up.

Carol was a friend of mine. She and I used to drink together back in the day when I was running the street. I sobered up but she stayed out there. I'd placed both her and Walter in the McLeod Hotel but they dropped out. Too many people died there, they told me.

Turns out, on the night she did herself in, Carol had mixed Valium and vodka. You can't OD on Valium alone, but if you mix it with alcohol, well, off you go. But how was anyone to know what Carol had taken when the cops led her out of the paddy wagon? I was told she was walking and talking. Not well, but no different than any other intoxicated client. An hour later she was dead. I wasn't on that night. I found out the next day. It hit me hard. When I stopped drinking I used to sit with her, usually around Van Ness where we had panhandled together. Her unwashed red hair, dulled from sleeping in Golden Gate Park, hung to her shoulders covering the holes in the collar of her jean jacket. She flashed me a smile, the lines in her face etched with dirt. Looking at her, I felt grimy, even woozy, like I was back doing it with her, like I had never cleaned up. It took a few seconds for that godawful feeling to leave but when it did, I was like so happy. I felt light and clean, the Bay breezes ruffling my shirt and my hair still damp from a shower that morning, and my mouth didn't taste of all kinds of stink from drinking, and it was hard to hold back how good I felt.

Carol would tell me how happy she was for me. But if she had wine, she'd always offer me a drink. If I said anything—you know, like, It was a long day today—she'd say, Here, have a drink. I'd not sit with her long. You don't go to a whorehouse for a kiss; you don't hang out with a drunk for their company if you're not drinking. I don't remember who told me that but it's true. I didn't want to slip. Still, I felt bad when I heard she died. Guilty somehow. Like because I'd gotten sober, she died alone. I would have died if I hadn't quit. I was glad I wasn't Carol, and that made me feel guilty too.

I watch Joe pause by each mat and notice a paperback sticking out of his hip pocket. He's a reader. He always has a book. With all his education and the fact he's a good ten years younger than me I'm guessing, I know he wouldn't look at me twice, but he's fun to watch. That ass. I'm sure he'd want to take a date to a club for a beer. Maybe not. Maybe after being around drunks all day at work the last thing he'd want is a drink. There's always Starbucks. That's what I'd tell him if he gave me the chance.

I tease Joe, call him a normie, you know, as in normal. He's a normal guy. He's not an alcoholic. He can have one drink and stop and not even think about it. When I was drinking, sometimes I'd stop after one just to prove I didn't have a problem, but I wanted a second drink and a third and a fourth and on and on. Hank says sobriety is a state of mind. That after so many years you can look at a billboard advertising some kind of booze and not think about it anymore than you would a car passing you on the road. I'm not there. I see a sign for booze and for a second it's like a contact high. I can feel it running through me.

I'm a little old for Joe, I know, but younger guys can like older women. Joe does little things like holding a door for me or he'll ask if I want a cup of coffee when he gets one for himself, and he'll walk me home if I don't have a ride. Not too many men look at me like a woman they would ask to walk home. His momma raised him right is all I'm saying. He stops at the door of the Bridge Hotel and I turn around and face him and that's when I think he should kiss me. He doesn't. Just says, See you at work tomorrow, Katie.

Sometimes, I dream of my ex, Matt, a heroin addict. We met in the Redwood City program. When he got out, he rented a room on the second floor of a house in the Richmond and sold plasma until he found a job working for a gay phone-sex company. I had just moved into Oliver House. On weekends, I'd request a pass and go over to his place. I'd show up in the morning and he'd still be in bed and I'd take off my clothes and crawl in with him.

The last time we were together, I heard him in the hall shower after I'd spent the night, and I decided to give him some love. I got out of bed, put on my robe and walked into the bathroom. I eased the shower curtain back, thinking I'd slip in and surprise him. I almost started laughing thinking how he'd jump in surprise, and I saw him standing under the water, back to me, tipping back a beer, and I jerked back almost falling. Matt spun around.

Goddamn, Katie! What are you doing?

I ran out the bathroom and into his room and started putting on clothes; Matt followed me dripping water.

Katie, it's not what you're thinking.

What is it I'm thinking, Matt?

It's just a beer. I can drink a beer.

He reached for me and I slapped him and his hand went up to his face and I pushed past him to the hall carrying my shoes.

Katie!

I hurried down the stairs and ran outside still holding my shoes, my hair all crazy from sleep like the fucked up, barefoot, homeless woman I once was.

He called here once late at night on his day off. Like two months ago. I answered and he said he saw a client he thought had been sober drinking in a club in the Haight. What do we do? he asked. I mean I thought she had cleaned up. I wondered if he had tried to pick her up and then recognized her and freaked out. Sometimes Carol and I would go to clubs on the first of the month when we got our general assistance checks. We'd drink with all the normies and get just as drunk as them. Guys would take us home. Be careful, girl, we'd say to each other. It was never great sex, kind of hurried and sloppy, and they'd get off not thinking too much about me. I waited for them to fall asleep. Then I'd wander their apartment, sit in the living room in the dark like it was my place. The shelf of paperback books. The kitchen sink cluttered with unwashed dishes. The framed prints with trees and inspirational sayings. I remember one: It always seems impossible until it's done—Nelson Mandela. I thought of that when I got sober, how I stared at those words written below pale mountains pressing against a purpling sunrise. Then I rinsed my mouth with toothpaste I found in his bathroom. I went back to the bedroom and smoothed out the sheets on my side of the bed. Not really my side. The side I slept on. Anyway, he didn't move. I didn't want to wake him. Would he remember me if he did? Probably. Maybe not at first but probably. Would he want me? Might. But it's weird because I wouldn't be drunk and I'd have this stranger on me with morning breath. Anyway, he didn't so much as move. I forgot what he'd been drinking. I eased out, closing the door behind me like I was never there.

I wonder if Joe had been drinking the night he called all upset about the client he saw drinking. I wonder who she was. Did he hit on her before he knew who she was? Joe can drink. He can hit on anybody he wants, I don't care. I mean I do but I don't. Maybe he's still at that stage where he can get wasted and still come to work. Maybe it's not a stage. Maybe he can do that the rest of his life. I don't know. I can't.

I lean back in my chair, watch Joe bend over each mat as he checks the detox clients. Tight jeans. It was at an AA meeting, I think, that I heard someone say you shouldn't get in a relationship at work during your first two years of sobriety, to avoid the kinds of stress that can send you back to drinking. But not working and no sex is another kind of stress. Been sober eighteen months. I got a job and I'm not drinking. No reason I shouldn't try my luck with a fuck buddy.

I see you watching that boy, Hank says.

What you saying?

Katie girl, you'd turn him inside out.

I'd go easy on him.

I gotta a wiggle a worm don't know nothing about if you need salvation.

Please!

Hank laughs. I think if I gave him the chance he'd jump on me in a minute. I don't like him in that way. I mean, I don't get that feeling in my chest looking at him as I do watching Joe. Hank's more like a big brother sort of. I don't know. He's not bad looking. He doesn't have an innocence about him like Joe does. There's a hardness to him, like a busy, unpaved road. He's thinking of leaving Fresh Start. Maybe taking a job at Walmart. He took it kind of serious what Tom said about moving on and swimming to shore and all that. He won't go back to school or anything, but a different job, a totally different job, might be a good thing. Leave the old life behind. Working here you're really not off the street, I get it. But you're sober. There's no forgetting your problems behind a bottle. I'm tired of dealing with people like my old self, drunks calling me names, cussing me out. Like they forgot we used to be on the street together. I get disgusted and beat up on myself for who I once was, like them, and they see my disgust and hate on me. I think Carol hated on me at times. Sometimes when she drank she'd turn mean. I'd never noticed that before, when I was drinking with her. But I sure noticed when I stopped and began doing her intakes. She'd tell me in a hoarse voice that sounded like she was not fully awake, We all got to die sometime. You think you won't? You think you're sober and that changes who you are? You're a drunk who ain't drinking. That makes no sense. I'm a drinking drunk. I ain't never going to quit. You can forget where you come from, Katie, but I won't.

Maybe another job would be good for Hank, but I think no matter where we go we'll always carry our old selves with us. We'll always be drunks, just not drinking drunks, so he might as well stay here. I will.

I squint to see Joe moving from mat to mat, the dim ceiling lights being no match for the shadows. At the table that Hank is sharing with Walter, he's again trying to drink coffee but his hands shake so bad he puts the foam cup on the table, and this time leans forward to drink from it like dog lapping from a puddle.

Joe stops by the mat with John Doe. He stares down and then bends over and leans in. After a moment, he drops to his knees and gets closer. Hank notices and comes up behind him. Joe stays down by the guy.

Everything all right? I shout.

Hank says something. Joe shakes his head. He stands. Hank kneels and leans in like Joe had. Joe watches Hank. Hank turns to him and raises his chin toward me. Joe comes over looking serious as a heart attack.

What's wrong? I ask.

The guy on mat two, Joe goes, voice shaking

What about him?

We don't think he's breathing.

Don't think he's breathing?

He's not breathing, Katie.

I stare at him and then I'm up and beside Hank. He holds two fingers against the guy's neck.

Talk to me, Hank, I say.

Nothing, he says. No pulse.

A blanket covers John Doe's legs. He smells of wood smoke and of poop, like he crapped himself in his sleep. Hank shakes his shoulder. He pumps his chest, one, two, one, two. The guy rocks like a log. His open eyes don't blink. Hank gets up pressing his hands against his knees like they hurt. He pulls the blanket over the guy's face. I swallow hard as if something's sticking in my throat.

He's already cold, Hank says.

You mean he's dead? Joe says, his voice almost cracking.

I still can't speak.

There was nothing wrong with him when I brought him in, Hank says. He was drunk that's all.

Hank didn't do anything wrong. I didn't either. Me and Hank got nothing to do with this. I was so used to fucking up and having to cover my ass when I was drinking that I didn't know what to do if something did go wrong. But this isn't that. I'm not drinking. This is just bad luck. For John Doe and no one else.

Poor guy, Hank says. I'll call Tom.

I'll call 911.

I can call it if you want.

I got it. You call Tom.

Hank lets out a deep breath. He doesn't move. He takes my hand and begins saying the serenity prayer. Joe watches us. God grant me the serenity to accept the things I cannot change, courage to change the things I can, and the wisdom to know the difference. When we finish, Hank squeezes my hand.

Sixty seconds at a time.

Back at you, I say.

I remember taking Valium one time after drinking a fifth of vodka with Carol. I don't know how many pills I took but Carol said, What are you doing? You want to kill yourself? She stuck her fingers down my throat and made me vomit. A fire burned in my throat as I retched, and the puke covered her fingers, but she kept them down my throat until I had nothing left. Carol wouldn't let me pass out. She said my soul would leave me and never come back. I'd be sleeping forever in darkness. She held my arms around my knees and rocked me back and forth and we stayed awake all night. A pain in my temples felt like screws being turned. My hands shook. Carol got us a mickey when Fred's Liquor opened at six. I held the bottle in both hands like a prayer and drank.

Most days, after a night in Golden Gate Park, Carol and I would work Van Ness, taking turns panhandling on the median near the intersection with Golden Gate. We had ourselves a cardboard sign we tore off a box we found in a dumpster: HOMELESS. ANYTHING WILL HELP. GOD BLESS. Carol had these markers from a shoulder pack a kid forgot at a bus shelter. Probably a kid. Had a blank spiral notebook in it with a few math problems scrawled in pencil like the kid was just getting used to writing. Simple stuff like $3 + 6 = 9$. I wondered what had happened. Was this one of those missing kids pictured on supermarket bags? What if it was? What if someone sees us with their pack? Carol thought I had a point and got rid of it, but she kept the markers. I used to draw, did you know that? she said. I shook my head. Well, I did, she said.

Carol took the lead with the sign while I waited across the street to relieve her. She'd hold it and when the light turned red she'd walk between idling cars and not say a word, just hold our sign. Sometimes, someone called her over and gave her a dollar or some change. Most times, people just stared over their steering wheels without blinking and ignored her. When she got tired or too warm in the sun, she gave me the sign and I took over. When it got really hot, we sat under the awning at a McDonald's and propped the sign up against the building. Usually we'd get enough for a couple of quarts of Thunderbird. One afternoon, we both passed out and someone stole my shoes. Had to have tugged them off my feet. I didn't feel a thing. I sat there my mouth tasting all kinds of foul from having slept after we shared a bottle, my body slick in its own oiled mess. Where're my shoes? I wondered. It just kind of hit me: I have no shoes. Someone took my shoes. I started laughing and then I got pissed. Carol lay on her side snoring, her head on our sign like it was a pillow. She had her shoes. Why'd someone take mine? I thought of taking hers. I thought and thought and then I did. I pulled them off her feet, gray sneakers that had once probably been white. They fit. A little tight but they fit. She kept on sleeping. She looked peaceful. Staring at her I tried to imagine us in a meadow. People walked past us, their knees level with my eyes. They stepped around us, and then I stood and they moved away, really skipped away like dancers, they didn't miss a beat, and then they resumed walking in a straight line again. Looking down at Carol, I said, I took your shoes. I knew taking her shoes, well, there's just something rotten about that. I didn't want to be that rotten but I was. I felt bad—not so bad as to give them back—but bad enough to say I'm going to detox. Hank checked me in. I took a shower and he gave me clean clothes, a yellow T-shirt and blue jeans, both of which were too big, and another pair of shoes. Sandals really but they fit better than Carol's shoes. I told him how I'd taken her shoes and I started crying. I hung on to them. I told myself I'd give them back when I got out of detox but I never did. I didn't have them with me when I saw her. And I didn't tell her I had taken them. I never mentioned them. About six months into my sobriety and about two months after I started working at Fresh Start, she died. The coroner had taken her body by the time I came into work. Funny the things you think of, but at the time my mind went back to the night I left her and how pebbles and bits of glass cut into the thin soles of her shoes. I could feel them dig in, like they were trying to get at my feet, and how I kept walking and hoped she'd yell for me so I'd turn around and go back and return her shoes.

I left a message for Tom, Hank says. He didn't pick up.

I put down my phone.

They said they're on their way, 911. Asked me if it was an emergency.

What'd you say?

Not anymore.

I glance around for Joe and see him sitting at the table with Walter. Hank and I go over and join them.

You ever seen a dead body? Hank asks Joe.

No.

Walter fingers an ashtray like maybe he could conjure up a smoke. Hank gives him one of his. Walter jams it in his mouth and Hank lights it for him. He stopped drinking cold turkey for a couple of months last year after he had a seizure. We had to refer him to San Francisco General. When he was released, he hung out at Fresh Start, stayed in our shelter at night. During the day, he volunteered, made coffee, and mopped the floors. What else could he do? No halfway house would take him, because he hadn't been through a program. No program would take him, because he had been through pretty much all of them. Besides, they all had long waiting lists. Maybe that's why he started up again. To have a purpose.

You know this guy, Walt?

Walter shakes his head.

He kind of looks like Rodney, I say.

Who's Rodney? Joe asks.

A-Rod? Walter says. No, it's not him.

He hangs around on Larkin, Hank says. Buys his wine at the convenience store on Eddy.

The blond guy, I say.

Yeah, Walter says. A-Rod, everyone calls him.

No, that's not him, Hank says.

That's I what I said, Walter says.

But it looks like him, I say.

He's not A-Rod, Walter says.

Who's A-Rod? Joe asks.

Joe asks if any of us want coffee. Me and Hank shake our heads. Walter nudges his cup forward and Joe takes it and walks to the counter. He's great eye candy but it's not going to happen between us. The way he walks me home, that's nice, I have to admit. I don't want to talk about how I'm not drinking all the time. Maybe if Hank got a job at Walmart he'd talk about something else. Maybe then I'd like him in the way I like Joe. It was good he said the serenity prayer. It kept my head straight. I liked that Joe took my hand at that moment.

I wonder what the dead guy thought this morning. If he knew he was sick, if he felt funny, funnier than normal. He was probably hungover. I imagine him in Golden Gate Park waking up, pulling his knees into his chest against the cold. He probably got up and rolled up his sleeping bag. Or maybe he just had blankets. They'd be wet with dew. He might have had a shopping cart. He may have hidden his gear behind bushes. That's what I did. That was me. It may not have been the dead guy at all.

We hear sirens and then the red lights of a squad car and an ambulance splash light against the windows. I get up and Hank follows me to the door. I open it to two officers. Three paramedics stand behind them in the shadows. One of the officers takes out a notepad. He has a heavy face and looks almost bored. His partner appears younger and stands to one side.

We got a call about a deceased person? Officer Notepad says.

Yes, I'm the one who called, I say.

Hank and I walk them over to John Doe. The heavy sound of their steps echoes off the concrete floor behind me. They glance at Walter, who stares down at the table, chin against his chest. I wonder if he has nodded off. The paramedics squat down and one of them pulls the blanket off John Doe's face. They stare at him.

How long has he been like this? one of them asks.

He came here about ten thirty tonight. We did a bed check at eleven and this is how he was, I say.

He was passed out on the street in front of the building, Hank says. He was breathing, too drunk to walk. Me and a volunteer brought him in.

The paramedics look at John Doe again.

Do you know who he is? one of them asks.

No, sir, I tell him.

Officer Notepad takes our names and phone numbers. One of the paramedics covers John Doe with the blanket again.

We'll call the coroner to pick up the body, one of them tells me.

If you get a name for him let us know, Officer Notepad says.

He and his partner walk back outside and sit in their squad car. The paramedics follow.

Hank picks up the clipboard and hands it to Joe.

Better go see that everyone else is breathing, he says.

Joe takes the clipboard. I watch him, not feeling a whole lot one way or the other.

I'll call Tom again, Hank says.

I'll miss Hank if he goes to Walmart. I think it'll be weird for him to work in a place with people who could never imagine a guy dying alone on a mat on the floor. Hank and I wouldn't have work to talk about anymore. I don't know what we'd have to say to each other. But we'd still have a lot in common. Too much. Maybe we're meant for each other after all.

Tom

Johnny wants to slam his burrito in my face. Wants to, will do, hard to read, but I'm leaning toward will do.

You took my job. Why don't you take my lunch too? Johnny snarls.

He's drunk, voice slurring in an ocean of saliva, jaws loose on their hinges. I just wanted a quick lunch. This little burrito joint run by a nice older lady, La Taqueria it's called, on the corner of Leavenworth and Ellis, its steamed windows marked with finger drawings by bored customers, the thick aroma of refried beans wafting from pots on a black stove that could use a good soap and water wipe-down, usually provides me a relaxed place to eat without anyone bothering me. A kind of break I can't get when I bring my lunch and eat in my office. Until Johnny showed up, I'd been sitting blissfully by myself.

He always drank but I never knew him to get this wound up. Of course, I'd not fired him before. We sat in my office two days ago, his eyes bloodshot and rheumy, pigeons on the windowsill, pacing back and forth, cooing, heads bobbing, witnesses to the hammer coming down on a guy I'd lied for and promoted.

Johnny, I said, you know how this works. When state budget cuts come down, I have to lay off staff. My way of doing things is to let go those people I think can find work. You can find work. You can get another job if you chill out on the drinking.

Over the last three years, I've laid off more staff than I want to think about. Fired. That's how it feels to them. The look in their eyes. The sense of betrayal. The tears. All the self-respect they had clawed back gone in the two or three sentences it takes for me to tell them. What did someone who had spent years on the street have other than the minimum-wage job I gave them? A room at a residential hotel, no kitchen, bathroom down the hall, and a tab at some restaurant that extended them credit, that's what. I laid them off and saw them back on the street in no time, back to what they'd known, back to the sidewalks, the doorways, the homeless shelters, in line with everyone else for whatever benefit they might be eligible for—general assistance, SSI, unemployment—blending in with one another in an undistinguished mass of ill-fitting thrift-store clothes in a poor version of a nine-to-five routine, as if they'd never left. In a way, I suppose, they hadn't.

This because of yesterday? Johnny asked.

Yes, I thought, it is. But instead I lied one more time to spare him the truth and to spare me his denials. Besides, our funding had been cut. That was no lie.

No, it's about the budget. It's about who I think can find a job.

I hated to fire Johnny. He was one of my guys I could rely on. But when the state slashed our funding, I had choices to make. My program coordinator, Don, found a new job. That saved some money but other staff still had to go. The way I saw it, a drinker like Johnny, who no matter how lit he gets can still make it to work on time and supervise the shelter, has a chance—I'm not saying a great one—of finding another job. That person, according to the skewed logic I engage in, should be laid off.

Is that it? Johnny asked.

I extended my hand and nodded.

I'm sorry, Johnny.

He wiped his eyes and looked away. He didn't believe me, I

knew. Too bad for him he ran into McGraw yesterday reeking of booze. Too bad McGraw knew he was on the clock. McGraw called me. You know Johnny smells like a brewery? I haven't spoken to him today, I lied. Well, he does, McGraw said, and now here we are.

I nodded and he left.

I want you to have my burrito, Johnny says again.

I'm trying to keep calm but I'm getting a little pissed off. How many times did Johnny show up to work smelling of booze? How many times did I talk to him about it? He used mouthwash, like that'd fool me or anyone. I looked the other way. I considered his drinking a perk I let him have because no matter what I could rely on him. He kept the train running, so to speak. But the staff and clients all knew he drank. They didn't say anything but they knew, and they knew I knew, and when I caught people nursing a bottle of Thunderbird in the shelter and told them to toss it or leave, they'd say, rightfully, What about Johnny? I had no good answer.

Johnny came to Fresh Start a year ago for a clothing referral. He wore an army fatigue jacket too big for his slim body. His graying hair hadn't been combed in a while and his missing front teeth left a gap in his mouth that made him hard to understand. He told me he'd been in the army, stationed in the Philippines. One morning, he was called into the office of his CO and told he was being discharged. The base was closing, he was no longer needed, the CO said. Johnny caught a flight out that night with nothing but his duffel bag. Twenty-four hours later, he landed in San Francisco, the closest US airport to the Philippines, or so he claimed.

What a crock of shit, I thought. The army doesn't discharge soldiers because a base closes. Johnny screwed up somehow. Maybe it was his drinking, I don't know. If I've learned anything

I've learned this: Don't believe what anyone on the street tells you. They have their secrets. They're not all bad or all crazy or all addicts. I've met more than a few who have nothing wrong with them. They need a job, that's it. I have to admit, I'm always blown away when not having a job turns out to be their only problem. But even then they have their secrets, their unbelievable tales to fill in the blanks of what they don't want you to know. I let Johnny have his story. I presumed he'd lost everything else.

While he stayed at the shelter, Johnny volunteered. He put mats on the floor, mopped the bathrooms, made coffee. When one member of the shelter staff quit, I offered his job to Johnny.

I really want you to have it, Johnny says again, tossing the burrito from hand to hand as if it were too hot to hold. I'll give you a fork and everything so you don't mess yourself.

Johnny takes a step toward me, trips, regains his balance. I hope something will distract him. People coming in for lunch. Something. To think that only a few months ago, I lied my way to hell to get Johnny the shelter supervisor job. At the time, the supervisor had been a guy from Texas we all called Tex. He seemed as normal and middle class as a bank teller, until one day he decided to resume his crack habit and I never saw him again. That created a job opening. I wanted Johnny to fill it.

However, I had hoops to jump through. My contract with the city doesn't allow me to appoint people to administrative jobs. Johnny and anyone else interested in the supervisor position had to appear before a three-member hiring committee made up of homeless men and women elected by people in the shelter to, according to the contract, give the homeless served by the agency a say in staffing. That in turn, or so the thinking went, would teach them responsibility. They'd be, in contract-speak, invested in the program and their own outcomes. The contract emphasized that the director could in no way influence the committee. I could sit in on interviews and help facilitate but I could not participate in discussions about the applicants or vote.

I posted the position and asked a homeless volunteer, a guy named Ross Hitchcock, to coordinate the election of a hiring committee. Ross grew up in Boston and has a thick New England accent. He had no teeth and when he wasn't talking, his mouth flattened into a thin line above his chin. He schemed and had a racket unique to anyone I knew. For several hours a day, he'd stand beside a parking meter and flag drivers searching for a parking space. He'd then offer to get them an hour on the meter in exchange for a quarter. If they agreed, he'd withdraw a popsicle stick from his pocket, jam it in the meter, crank it up and down, and watch the numbers flip until they reached sixty minutes. Pleased and amused by his ingenuity, drivers would often give Ross additional change. Within a few hours, he'd make a few bucks.

Ross announced the election that night at the shelter. Whoever wanted to run wrote their name on a piece of paper tacked by the front door. More than a few people thought the candidate sheet was the sign-in list for a bed. As a result, we had many clients unaware they were running for the committee. Three days later, I left ballots with the names of dozens of candidates by the front desk. Completed ballots were put in a box. The three candidates who received the most votes moved on. If they showed up for the interviews, we had a hiring committee. If they didn't, we held another election.

The day of the vote, I called Johnny into my office and told him I wanted him to be the new super.

You can't go before the hiring committee with alcohol on your breath, I warned him.

I don't drink when I'm working.

You drink and everyone knows it, period. If you want the job, don't come here smelling of booze.

At first, only Johnny put in for the job. Then the day before the application deadline, one other staffer applied. Billy White. He had come to the shelter about the same time as Johnny. He had a wide, open face with a mole on his right eyelid that seemed not to bother him, but always distracted me whenever we spoke. Guys would hit him up for money and he'd give them what little he had and then act surprised when no one paid him back. If someone said, Hey, Billy, I like that sweater, he'd lend it to them, but of course he never got it back, and I'd see him at night in line waiting for the shelter to open, his arms crossed, shivering, the hurt expression of a child who knew he had been taken advantage of but didn't understand how or why writ large across his face. I hired Billy to get him away from the piranhas feeding off him.

He did not make my life easy. He never got to work on time, because he insisted on standing up to the indignities of his life, as if, now with a job, he could finally assert himself against those who had abused his trust. One time, he blamed his tardiness on his landlord. That morning, he refused to pay rent after he had complained about the halls being dirty, and nothing was done about it. The landlord threatened to evict him. Billy then called lawyers to sue the owner. Then he asked other lawyers to sue those lawyers for not taking his case. When they refused, he walked to the San Francisco Chronicle to ask a reporter to write about the dirty halls. He demanded a meeting with the editor. He waited a long time before his request was denied. Had they not made him wait, he explained, he wouldn't have been late.

I kept him. Firing Billy would have been like kicking a puppy. Fresh Start existed for the Billys of the world, and the Johnnys and Texes too; people who, we should concede, will never fit into the five-day workweek. Unless, of course, our work ethic changes and allows for people who talk to other people none of us can see, people with twenty-four-seven drinking and drug problems, people like Billy who obsess on the smallest slight, people with college degrees who look good on paper, but have troubles too, and have ended up on the street among all the other dispossessed in an equal-opportunity smorgasbord of tri-aged men and women, unable to get past the gated entrance to the American Dream.

About two weeks after Tex vanished, Johnny and Billy appeared before a hiring committee made up of clients I knew well:

Charles, a speed freak, a tall, lean man in his late thirties, was on one of his periodic sober runs. He could sing like nothing else mattered in a voice that should have had Berry Gordy knocking at our door.

Gill Harlee, a barrel-chested guy with a huge laugh; a round, bowling-ball stomach; and an explosive temper. A meaningless disagreement on something as simple as the weather could set him off and lead to fights. Good mood or bad, he always shouted as if he was trying to make himself heard above insurmountable noise.

Marcela Brooks, a woman who came in every morning for coffee, who we all called Granny because of her age. Depending on the day, she'd tell us she was seventy-eight or ninety. She wrapped herself in at least three coats and used a wheelchair like a walker, hobbling behind it and pausing every so often to catch her breath, her lined face canyoned with exhaustion.

On a Wednesday afternoon, the committee interviewed Johnny first. We sat in a circle by a closet where we stored the mats. We held a list of ten questions. The sun shone and I could see seagulls circling above a YMCA at the corner of Golden Gate and Leavenworth. Johnny took a chair next to mine. I smelled the alcohol on his breath.

First question:

Charles: What would you do if the shelter was full and someone needed a place to stay at two in the morning? Would you turn them away?

No, Johnny answered. He'd find them a spot even if it meant sitting in a chair. Granny asked a similar question about a family that showed up in the middle of the night. Johnny said he wouldn't bother calling other shelters. He understood we weren't a family shelter, but at that hour a family would need rest, especially the kids. He'd take them in too.

God bless the children, Granny said, and then launched into a story about how she was denied shelter by the Salvation Army because she refused to take a shower.

That wasn't right, she said. A shelter's not supposed to turn people away. I'm an old woman.

After we finish here, Granny, you and I will talk about it, I said.

It wasn't right what happened to me, Granny insisted.

I turned to Charles and Gill.

Let's continue, I said.

What about me? Granny said.

We'll talk, I said.

Second question:

Gill: What would you do if . . . Gill stopped and put the list of questions aside. Instead, he asked Johnny if he'd kick someone out of the shelter if they were caught drinking or using. Before he could answer, Gill demanded, What about you? Would you eighty-six yourself?

What do you mean?

You come to work drunk.

I don't drink here, Johnny said.

Gill smirked.

Do you attend AA, Johnny? Charles asked.

No, Johnny said.

Would you go to AA if you get this job?

I don't see why I would, Johnny said. I don't drink at work.

Let's stick to the questions, I said, raising the list.

Gill made a face and his hand shook with mounting anger, but he didn't explode. I appreciated his self-control. Still, he'd done some damage.

Billy showed up fifteen minutes late. He couldn't find his keys, he explained. As excuses went, that was so acceptably mainstream he left me speechless.

First question:

Charles: If it's raining outside, would you open the shelter earlier than usual?

Billy scrunched up his face, thinking. He wanted to know the situation of each person seeking shelter. Had they ever been eighty-sixed? Were they intoxicated? Were other shelters available to them? The committee made up answers to his hypotheticals until I intervened, contract be damned.

Billy, just answer. It's a yes-or-no question.

Then yes, he said, although I think these questions need to be more specific.

When we finished interviewing Billy, I walked him to the door, closing it behind him.

What do you all think? I asked.

Johnny, the committee agreed, was the better applicant. He answered the questions with common sense. They'd seen him on the job. They knew he was reliable. Billy, they worried, would complicate the simplest problem. They worried he'd obsess over one task at the expense of others. However, Johnny's drinking disturbed them more. Whatever else could be said about Billy, he wouldn't be drunk when he enforced the rules about alcohol and drugs.

Why do you allow Johnny to work with alcohol on his breath? Charles asked me.

I've always wondered that myself, Gill said.

I didn't answer. My overriding principle: Make a bad situation less bad. Johnny was my less bad.

Because we're here for people with problems and despite all of his, he works out better than most.

They didn't disagree. However, whatever their own problems, Charles, Gill, and Granny understood hypocrisy. They voted for Billy.

Now, are we going to talk about me getting thrown out of the Salvation Army? Granny asked.

Billy, I knew, would be a disaster. I needed a plan. Crisis fueled quick thinking. I reminded the committee that according to the contract, the ED had to sign off on all new hires. I knew McGraw wouldn't care who I hired. I just had to tell him. I didn't. Not yet. Instead, I called the committee back for a meeting the next day and commenced to tell them one bald-faced lie after another. I told them that I'd met with McGraw and he had recommended hiring both Billy and Johnny. He wanted one of them to supervise the day program, the other the night shelter. It would provide for better coverage to split the position into two.

Granny and Gill liked the idea. Only Charles objected.

What's the point of having a hiring committee if McGraw's just going to make his own decision? he asked.

He didn't decide, I said. He just gave us another idea. Think about it. This will open up two staff positions.

Charles, I knew, wanted a job. It served my purpose to dangle the possibility now. I couldn't tell if he picked up on my not-so-subtle hint, but he didn't push his objection. The contract could talk about homeless people participating in decision-making all it wanted but everyone knew who was in charge. McGraw. The committee had its say. By channeling McGraw and offering a bribe, I had mine.

As I figured, McGraw didn't care. He thought it was a little cumbersome having two supervisors, but if that's what I wanted, fine. I gave him some mumbo jumbo about how it was an example of the agency taking a job opening and creating more than just one opportunity. He gave that laugh again and slapped me on the shoulder. He liked how that sounded. Funders would eat it up. McGraw got his talking point. The committee got Billy. I got Johnny. Win-win-win.

I gave Johnny days and Billy nights. There wouldn't be much to do at night once the lights went out at eight, which I thought would suit Billy best. Johnny worked out as I knew he would. Boozy breath, but fine. Billy, however, was Billy.

I'm sorry I'm late, Billy would apologize to me. The bus was running behind schedule. And I talked to the driver about how that wasn't right, and he talked back to me. So I wouldn't get off until he apologized.

I'd listen. I always listened. Billy's outrage at everyday insults that the rest of us took for granted I found endearing. Soon however, the tardiness got out of hand and I suspended him for two days, but it didn't make an impression. Finally, I dropped him down to shelter staff again. He didn't object. OK, he said. The dejected look on his face told me he didn't understand that I didn't appreciate his need to confront life's every disparaging moment.

He was so preoccupied with standing up for his wounded dignity that the demands of being a supervisor had, I think, become just one more humiliation. Whatever he felt didn't matter. I got what I'd wanted all along. Johnny was now in charge. No one asked me about filling Billy's position and I didn't offer.

About two weeks later, McGraw called me into his office. He sat at a long table strewn with files and spreadsheets, glasses perched at the tip of noise. A computer glowed behind him and a shelf behind his head held books about time management. I knocked on his open door. He looked at me, dragged a hand through his mop of blond hair and laughed a here-we-are-in-the-shitstorm laugh that I knew couldn't be good. He pointed to a chair. I sat down. Then he got to it. Another budget cut. This time the state had decided not to renew a homeless adult programs grant that, among other things, covered some of my staff's salaries. I'd have to cut some positions and combine others.

Start at the top, McGraw said. Higher the salary the better.

I knew what that meant. In the pecking order of high salaries I was first, Johnny second. Well, I knew I wasn't going to lay myself off. McGraw looked at me over his glasses, gave that laugh again, and went straight to the nut cutting.

I saw Johnny this morning. He smelled like a brewery. You have to draw some lines.

If I draw lines, I'll fire everybody.

Johnny came to work drunk. There's your line.

Now that I'd drawn it, Johnny had nothing to lose going off on me in La Taqueria. I watch him take another unsteady step toward my table. I look at the guy behind the register. He's adding up receipts and doesn't notice a thing. Whatever's going to happen, I guess, will happen. I push back in my chair but remain seated. If I stand, Johnny might think I'm gearing up for a fight. Don't be the aggressor. De-escalate. Where'd I learn that? Some staff development. Strange what goes through your head when you think a burrito is about to wallpaper your face.

I don't want it, Johnny, I say again.

He sways and grabs the back of a chair. He drops the burrito on a table and sits sloppily in the chair. Stares at the floor, chin against his chest, arms loose at his sides as if something essential had left him. Saliva hangs off his mouth in a thin line, and he closes his eyes until I assume he's nodded out.

Johnny, I say. Johnny.

I smell it before I notice Johnny pissing himself, a slow, wet stain unfurling across his crotch.

Johnny, Jesus, wake up!

I get up and shake his shoulder. He opens his eyes slowly, looks lost, confused. He closes them again and I keep shaking him.

Johnny.

He turns his head and stares bleary-eyed, sagging deeper in his chair.

What? he says, his voice burdened by the effort to speak, rising out of his throat in a cracked whisper.

Before I can say anything, he presses a hand against the table and rises seemingly half asleep. He reels over the table like a bop bag, turns slowly, and walks out stiff-legged, arms out for balance, angling through the open door to the street. Through the fogged windows, I see the outline of his body pass in staggering steps. The odor of piss rises off his chair. I was sure I'd take a burrito to the face. I hadn't expected it to end this way. In the words of my contract, a positive outcome. Staring out the door, I remind myself that Johnny was just another layoff, nothing personal. He brought it on himself. I covered for him until I no longer could but as much as I want to, I can't rationalize away the guilt I feel wrapped tight and tucked away deep inside me and out of reach most days. I stand beside his chair a moment longer, then reach for the burrito and drop it into my coat pocket. Someone in the shelter will eat it.

Walter

I'm in the driveway of Oliver House in my sweats balancing my right foot against the security gate stretching for a four-block jog that's really like a fast walk I do every night. I keep my leg straight and try to touch my forehead to my knee.

A man pushes three shopping carts heaped with crushed cans and empty bottles up Masonic Avenue toward the center. The carts are tied together, clanking loudly, and form a train like miniature freight cars. Three bloated trash bags filled with more cans and bottles hang from each cart. The man leans into his load, head down, arms outstretched and locked at the elbows. I raise my chin and he nods. Looks like he's heading into the Haight. Likely will crash in Golden Gate Park. I've slept there more than a few times my own self. Man, just thinking about sleep makes me tired. Yawning, I look at my watch.

Five o'clock, but it's December and already dark. A full pock-marked moon throws a silvery blue light over the street. Stars snap in and out of the sky like fireflies. My body must get fooled somehow by the early night, because although it's early I'm beat and want to crash. Curfew starts at nine, but I'll crawl into the sack by seven and sleep until morning. If I wake up in the middle of the night, I'll heat some milk.

A warm glass of milk helps you sleep, my counselor told me when I first got here.

My bunkmate says anything white should go in your arm. I'm

hip, I tell him, and we laugh. Our counselors warned us both against that kind of stinkin' thinkin', even as a joke.

Last week, my counselor suggested I take up running.

Exercise'll give you energy, he said. You spend too much time in your room.

It's been two weeks since some guy died here and my name came up on the waiting list. The guy had a seizure. Fell out of his chair in an AA meeting, eyes wide open, staring at the ceiling. At least that's what I was told when I was in detox at Fresh Start. So I got his bed.

This is your last chance, Walter, Katie told me. I had to do major arm twisting to get you in. Don't screw up this time.

The man pushing the carts stops at the house next door. He takes off his sweatshirt and ties it around his waist, wiping his face with his undershirt. I can see his breath. Two brown shopping bags piled in a blue recycling tub near a station wagon rattle with bottles as he picks them up and hefts them into the rear cart. The right rear wheel of the station wagon straddles the curb. Faded bumper stickers pasted on the back read TAKE IT EASY and ONE DAY AT A TIME.

Say! Say! Get away from there! Get away from my car! a man shouts from an open door at the house next door.

Cart Man freezes for an instant, cocks his head trying to see who's shouting at him. Then he quickly sorts through the remaining cans and bottles in the tub.

Get away! the man next door shouts again, switching on the porch light. Someone broke into my car, goddamn it, now get the hell away! It was you or some other street son of a bitch, wasn't it? You bastard. I should have you arrested. Now get away from my car.

The man steps out onto the porch holding a steaming mug in one hand, the other hand cupped over his eyes. He's got on a suit with a tie draped around his neck. His clothes look like he slept in them.

It was probably one of you bastards, he says, giving me a look. You and your halfway house. Goddamn drunks all of you. I know.

He sets the mug down on a patio chair. I look away and start stretching my left leg, glancing at him when I think he won't notice.

I see you out here running, the man says. It was probably you. A no-good drunk busting into people's cars. I know. I said this would happen when they built your goddamn center.

I stare at the ground and try to touch my toes. The moon lights up everything. Brick houses and trim lawns, telephone poles and power lines, fence posts and empty lots. Wet leaves lie scattered over the street curled in puddles.

The man next door walks stiffly to the station wagon stopping at the driver's side. He bends over, peers in. The man with the carts follows him, nods at me to come over. I go to the passenger side.

The radio's missing, see? the man from next door says.

None of the windows are broken. The radio is gone but the interior isn't damaged. A wallet lies on top of a coat on the passenger seat. I think I should say something, but I don't need this guy in my face any more than he already is. My heart gets to racing. I become angry fast. My counselor says it's because alcohol has fried all my nerves.

You think I did that? I say tapping a window. How the hell did I get in?

The man gets quiet, looks genuinely puzzled, and considers the window like he's never seen it.

All right, maybe it wasn't you, he concedes. But it was someone. Someone must have had one of those things tow companies use to open locked cars. One of those sticks they slide down the door and snap open the lock.

You'll find your radio in a pawn shop, I say.

You wouldn't get much for it. I know pawn shops, he says, opening the door and reaching under the front seat. The radio was one of those removable kinds. I always put it under the front seat but it's not there.

He has trouble standing back up and leans heavily on the door. His breath smells of coffee and booze and for a second I feel light-headed. I wouldn't call it a contact high, but the smell sure put me back on Sixth Street at Fred's Liquor Store.

The man pushes past me and walks back to his porch, leaning a little to one side.

At least they didn't take your wallet, I tell him.

He turns around, holding his mug.

What's that?

He comes back to the car and sets his mug on the roof. I point at the passenger seat and he opens the door and grabs his wallet. He picks up his coat too, revealing a small, square, black radio beneath it. He hesitates, holding his wallet and coat.

Goddamn radio, how'd it get there?

He opens his wallet, makes a show of counting his money and credit cards, but his fingers shake and he drops the wallet on the pavement. I hand it back to him.

I always put it under the seat.

I didn't take it.

I know. I'm sorry for what I said earlier. I respect what you're doing, getting sober. Really. I know. How long's it been?

Not long.

But it feels long?

Yeah. Yeah, it does.

That's how I felt. I made fifteen years. Fifteen. Jesus. It got too long for me and I just fell off. Man, I stopped drinking, made my meetings and then I just fell off and now I'm messing up.

He looks away and I see his eyes tearing up.

Look at me. I couldn't find my goddamn radio under my goddamn coat. Christ. Don't you just hate yourself sometimes?

I don't know about that. I wouldn't say hate. Not yet anyway.

Wait'll you do the fourth step, the man says. Wait'll you start making amends. You'll see.

He sniffles and I hear Cart Man pushing his load away from the curb. The rusted wheels grate on their axles and the bottles and cans click, clack, click as he moves forward.

The man doesn't pay him any attention. He holds his mug in one hand and jams the radio, coat, and wallet under his other arm. He's still a little weepy.

You take care, he says. Take it easy.

I begin stretching again. I reach for my toes, trying to keep my knees locked. Then I straighten and twist from side to side, faster and faster. I lean back and roll my head. Stars explode when I blink my eyes.

Fifteen fucking years, I think. Fifteen. Jesus.

I start running. I pass Cart Man and a woman walking her dogs. A bus stops at Haight and Masonic and I listen to traffic somewhere far away. I splash through muddy puddles that stain my pants as I pick up my pace. I pump my arms harder. Moonlight carves the street into shifting, jagged shapes. Leaves stick to my shoes. The sound of my running bounces off houses, my breath coming in gasps until the ache in my chest is too much. I stop, bend over, hands on my knees, sucking in air. I hear Cart Man behind me and look back. I see the dark outline of the carts approaching, hear the noise of the cans like the tolling of bells, and I watch my neighbor walking up the porch steps, one hand on the railing. He looks out at the street like someone stranded on shore. He backs up, switches off the outside light, enters the darkness of his house, and closes the door. I hear it shut. The night closes around me and I start running again.

Tom

Raymond lost Martin's money.

What are you talking about?

Laird goes: Martin told me. Raymond told him and then Martin told me. I still buy him breakfast, you know, to make sure he eats, and we talk.

Getting Martin breakfast, that's really nice of you, I say. Have him over to your bachelor pad, do you? You cook those Egg McMuffins yourself?

Laird ignores my dig. He had sort of adopted Martin. At least that's what he wanted people to think. Like he was Martin's Mother Teresa. Look at me. Look at how I'm doing more for Martin than anybody else. Then Raymond stepped in and did for Martin what Laird hadn't, and he didn't boast about it either. Raymond's a minister. He preaches on Sundays at a storefront church a few blocks south of here near Civic Center Park. Not some guy with a matchbook degree, but a real minister with a real degree from the University of San Francisco hanging above his desk inside a frame nice enough to know he didn't buy it at Walgreens. That frame and diploma are the only unhumble things about Raymond.

Raymond was handling Martin's money through a friend at a bank, Laird says. You didn't know that?

I don't answer. I look up at the sky, feel the sun on my face, and let out a long breath. Of course I knew. Everyone knew. Martin talked.

I got a meeting with McGraw, I tell Laird.

I don't really. I just want to get away from Laird. It's barely past nine in the morning. I got in ten minutes ago. I need coffee. Lots of coffee.

I already told McGraw, Laird says and gives me this smirk. But don't worry. I didn't tell him how much. What was it? Ten, fifteen thousand? More? I'll leave it to you to tell him that. I don't want to make you look bad.

Another maddening smirk.

I don't have anything to look bad about, I say.

I feel Laird watch me go. I keep walking down Leavenworth toward McGraw's office and make like I'm buzzing the bell to be let in the door but I'm really looking out the corner of my eye at Laird. I have enough to do without worrying about him. Raymond supervises the shelter and drop-in center. Until recently, he answered to Don, my program coordinator, but Don got hired by the AIDS Foundation right before I was going to lay him off. If Don was still here this would be on him to fix. But he's not here. So now I got to deal with Laird. And McGraw. Son of a bitch. You picked a good time to go, Don.

Laird crosses the street to a convenience store. This speed freak we all call Big Pete hits Laird up for money, but Laird shrugs him off. Laird's not into speed freaks. He likes to make out like he helps the Martins of the world. They're more sympathetic than speed freaks jonesing on the sidewalk. He likes to act high and mighty with speed freaks. Get all NA in their face.

As soon as Laird walks into the store, I hurry back to Fresh Start without coffee. Raymond's sitting at his desk, back to the door, staring out a window at a boarded-up building, his Bible open on his lap. In the alley separating a vacant building from the shelter, pigeons fly past, flapping loudly in the dim light.

Laird knows, I tell Raymond.

Raymond ignores me, reads aloud from the Bible: The Lord is my light and my salvation; whom shall I fear? The Lord is the stronghold of my life; of whom shall I be afraid? Though an army encamp against me, my heart shall not fear; though war rise up against me, yet I will be confident.

Put the Bible up, Raymond. Laird knows your buddy walked with Martin's money.

Raymond raises his head and without turning around says, Laird was just up here.

What did he say?

That Martin told him I lost his money.

And what did you say?

I told him what happened.

Why?

It was the truth, Raymond says.

I watch a pigeon strutting back and forth on the ledge of a broken window puffing its chest at another pigeon.

The truth? Jesus, Raymond, fuck the truth. We're talking about our jobs here.

Goddamn Laird. He's one of these formerly homeless guys who get off the street, rent a room somewhere, and spend all their time around places like Fresh Start pretending to help other homeless guys when really, they're just living off Social Security and doing nothing more than what they did when they were homeless: hanging out on the street.

Laird said that before he was homeless, he used to be a manager for an AT&T office in the financial district until his marriage went south and he went all to hell. I don't know. The guy can't spell worth a lick, and his teeth are as crooked as a boxer's nose. Small red blotchy mushroom clouds dot his face like something exploded beneath his skin. The result of a childhood allergy, he tells anyone who asks.

I don't ask questions, but I wonder: Wouldn't an AT&T office manager know how to spell and have dental insurance and maybe see a doctor for his face? It seems to me more must have happened than a loused-up marriage to go from the financial district to the street just like that. If he ever worked in the financial district.

What I do know is that every time Laird sees one of my staff fuck up, he runs in and rats them out to their supervisor. He used to rat them out to me until he realized I didn't really care one way or the other that so-and-so was late one day, or that so-and-so had cussed out a client, or that so-and-so took a longer than usual lunch break. This would never be allowed at AT&T, Laird would say.

Well, motherfucker, I told him one time, you're not at A fucking T and T anymore, are you? You're in the Tenderloin. We hire the goddamn homeless and a lot of them have done nothing but drink from nine to five since whenever and now they got a lot to learn. With all your office management experience, Laird, do you want to teach them the fine art of working for a living? And by the way, Laird, what exactly do you do now?

That put the brakes on Laird knocking on my door ragging about my staff. At least I thought it had.

There's nothing I can do now but go see McGraw, I tell Raymond. For both our sakes.

Raymond nods.

An uneasy quiet settles between us, interrupted by the cooing of the pigeons. I look around the empty shelter. Not much to it. A meal and an army cot for the night. Open seven at night, kick everyone out the next morning by six, and send them over to the drop-in and the jobs counselor. A lot of the guys just sit around all day until the shelter opens again. Pretty simple. But then Raymond helped Martin and it got all kinds of complicated.

Raymond told me he had it all worked out. The bank teller was a good friend and would handle Martin's money so Martin wouldn't get ripped off. Then a week ago he told me his buddy had walked with Martin's money. Raymond said he would find the guy and get it back. I should have fired Raymond then and saved my ass, but I didn't. I just wanted Raymond to do what had to be done and for the whole thing to go away.

I screwed up. Listen to your gut. I listened to Raymond instead. I knew we should have stayed away from Martin's money. Shoulda, coulda, woulda. But for a moment I thought we could actually help Martin. Martin, whom we'd all given up on. That this time we'd actually get him off the street, like we had tried to do so many times before. Raymond had a plan. Something none of us had thought of before. It made a lot of sense.

So I guess I did listen to my gut.

Before you see McGraw, Raymond says, you should know that Laird said he was going to file a complaint.

What kind of complaint?

A complaint about us to the grievance committee of the board of directors. About how we handled Martin's money.

We?

You and me.

Shit. I knew about the bank, but I didn't know your friend would walk with Martin's money.

I think knowing about the bank is the same as handling his money, Raymond says.

We got to stick together, I say, ignoring the sour look Raymond's giving me. I'm going to McGraw. What I'll do is tell him you're going to pay Martin back. I'll say: Raymond will set it right. I'll tell him how good your work has been and maybe I can convince him to suspend you and no more. Suspension without pay for a week or something. That's a pinch but it beats being fired.

The Lord detests lying lips, but he delights in men who are truthful, Raymond says. The poorest of the poor will find pasture, and the needy will lie down in safety. But your root I will destroy by famine; it will slay your survivors.

I don't know what you mean by that, Raymond. I really don't. I'm trying to save your job and mine. Whatever happens, you got to leave my name out of it. If I'm caught up in this, I can't back you. Then it's the old every-man-for-himself routine.

I reach across his desk to shake his hand. A bunch of pigeons flap past, breaking the tension, and I step back at the noise and drop my hand.

For the righteous falls seven times and rises again, but the wicked stumble in times of calamity, Raymond says.

Goddamn, more Bible talk. Like I told him, I knew about the bank but I didn't know the bank teller would walk. That's the truth. I don't care what Raymond thinks. And if he can't think clearly, he'd better start looking on the employment page of Craigslist. Because if he thinks I'll back him at the risk of my own job when all he can do is quote the Bible, well, then so much for thinking.

I leave Raymond's office and walk outside. The fog remains heavy and drips form along my face, pushed by the wind. Big Pete is still outside the drop-in trying to shake down staff for smokes. His dope-fiend partners Ross and Jim are with him scratching their arms like they have fleas. They used to work in the shelter before they started using again. Clean for five years, then boom, got the itch. Now they make no sense. Their minds are rattled like someone shaking a jar filled with marbles.

I cross my arms against the cold and lean against the shelter building. A rat scurries along the curb and I almost jump out of my skin. I slump against the building again, heart pounding. Sometimes, I wonder when I lost it. I don't know. I don't. I remember as a teenager, I backed into a car and broke one of its taillights. I had just gotten my license. I left a note on the windshield with my name and number. I told my father, thinking he'd be all kinds of proud of how I took responsibility, but instead he read me the riot act about how the owner of the car would call and take us to the cleaners for every nick and scratch. I was sixteen and the old man made an impression. You get raised to do the right thing and tell the truth, but not if it might bite you in the ass. That's the message. Whether I learned that then or learned it later and just think I learned it then, I can't say.

I should have known Raymond, being a minister and all, would cause problems. I hired him last year. His first day on the job he taped a piece of paper above his desk with this on it: There will always be poor people in the land. Therefore I command you to be openhanded toward your brothers and toward the poor and needy in your land. Deuteronomy 15:11.

Well, if God commanded that Raymond take on Martin, he gave him a tough assignment. Martin's a big old bald-headed crazy bastard, maybe about fifty. He dresses in black and wears a winter coat streaked with bird shit no matter how warm the weather. He talks to himself for long stretches at a time. Whatever he's hearing inside his head tears him up. He'll sit giggling in a corner unaware of how much he sweats and stinks by wearing that heavy coat. He carries bags of salt and pours the salt in his mouth like normal guys would peanuts. The counselors in our mental health program refer him to San Francisco General every now and then. The doctors tranq him and he comes back to the drop-in doing the Thorazine shuffle.

Then one day Laird stepped in all high and mighty with his AT&T bullshit. Saying how we got to do this, that, and the other for Martin. Do an intervention, he said. We can't just sit back and let the man eat salt. We have to intervene.

Well, goddammit, Laird, I said, intervene then. You go and take on this guy and hold his hand and put him on every goddamn waiting list around for this and that halfway house and see just what the fuck you can do for him. And if you do get him in somewhere, how long do you think he'll stick? How long do you think it will be before he stops taking his meds and wanders off? You think we haven't tried, Laird? You think Martin hasn't sampled the hospitality of several halfway houses after weeks and weeks of effort on our end? I tell you what, Laird. I've been doing this job for fourteen years. We're done trying, Laird. We got a good little routine now with Martin. He hangs in the drop-in and eats his salt, and we give him a shelter bed. Works for Martin. Works for me.

Laird complained to McGraw, who was busy making appointments with some suits downtown about the youth program. Kids are good for fundraising. People care about kids, the younger the better. They're like puppies. People don't care about homeless adults. They're not puppies. I can just see McGraw listening to Laird and noticing his fucked-up yellow teeth and how he spits a little when he talks. McGraw's a flowchart guy. Information flows from the bottom box to the box above it and from that box to the next higher box. He's the top box. Laird skipped some boxes going directly to McGraw. McGraw doesn't like to see the flow interrupted. He sent Laird back down the chart to me and I sent him further down to Raymond. McGraw didn't follow up and neither did I.

Then someone from the mayor's office called about Martin. I could only guess Laird had complained to somebody at city hall. I told the someone who called that Martin was seeing our counselors on a daily basis, that he used the drop-in center during the day and slept in the shelter at night, and the someone said, I see, and we both hung up.

Never heard another thing from the mayor's office or from Laird either. He had done his thing. He had stirred up his little shit and convinced himself of his power. Not that he didn't care about Martin. On a scale of one to ten, I'd say Laird was about a two, because, as he said, he would get Martin breakfast.

Raymond however was a ten and then some. He took Martin on like a mission.

I stay standing outside the shelter trying to clear my head. Trying to think. How do I tell McGraw we lost all of a crazy homeless guy's money? I won't. I can't. My legs feel locked at the knees. I don't want to move, but I got to. I got to get on and deal with McGraw. Better me going to him than him calling me in.

I walk toward the admin building, each step an effort. Then it hits me and I stop so fast I almost fall over. A way I can tell McGraw that Raymond lost Martin's money but that we won't have to pay it back. Raymond will have to be the fall guy for this to work but he's the one who got us into this mess. What else can he expect? Payback's a bitch. I got it almost worked out when I hear Big Pete calling me.

Pete's about as wide as the block and more than six feet tall. He's always moving, little darting moves like he's trying to fake someone out. At the same time his head bops around like one of those little dolls you see on the dashboard of a taxi, but he's retained his muscle somehow. Hands thick as bricks. When he fights, his fists emerge from the long sleeves of his frayed trench coat like something shot out of a cannon. We don't allow him in the drop-in or the shelter, because one time, for no reason, he kicked someone's ass so bad the guy nearly died.

Hey, man, Pete says, jogging across the street, coat flapping around his waist. Jim and Ross watch him.

What's up, Pete?

It's all good, you know that.

He laughs, puts on his sunglasses and leans down by my ear like we have some secret deal going on.

You help me out, man? Loan me a dollar?

I like that. Loan. I reach into a hip pocket for the change I keep on me so I don't have to pull out my wallet. I always give Pete money when he asks for it. I'd rather do that than have him coldcock me for my wallet. Jim and Ross stretch their necks out trying to see how much I hand him. Four quarters. Pete takes it without a word.

One morning several months back, after everyone had been kicked out of the shelter, Raymond came to me and said, We got to get Martin on disability so he can get a place to live. I told him the last time we tried to get Martin on disability was about three years ago. He was denied because of an obsession he had at the time with trash. He used to pick up bits of paper on the sidewalk outside the drop-in for no other reason than he got a kick out of doing it. No matter how small, Martin picked it up and threw it away, talking to himself the entire time. Sometimes, he just shoved the bits of paper in his coat pocket. I'm not going to say the sidewalks were much cleaner, but they weren't as cluttered, I'll give him that.

When the disability people came out to interview Martin, they saw him doing his thing with trash and were impressed but in the wrong way. They said Martin's trash fixation showed he cared about his community. Therefore he was not all that nuts. Therefore he could find a paying job like janitorial work. Therefore he didn't need disability.

The book of Proverbs says, If you mistreat the poor, you insult your creator, Raymond said when I finished telling him the story.

What's that supposed to mean?

That failure does not excuse us from doing nothing, Raymond said.

I didn't stand in his way. I figured Martin would be denied and Raymond would find another Bible quote and move on. What I hadn't counted on was that by then, Martin had some things going for him. He had stopped picking up trash. Instead, he had started eating salt. The disability people stared slack-jawed as Martin ground mouthfuls of salt instead of answering their questions. Raymond stood behind him, Bible in hand.

Whether it was through God's intervention or the salt, Martin got his disability. Not only did he get it, his start date was rolled back to his original disability application three years earlier. Crazy Martin got $21,600 dropped in his lap just like that, plus the start of a regular monthly check of six hundred dollars.

Laird was stewed, man. He gave Raymond looks that Ray Charles could have seen were so full of hate that they'd have made even Muhammad Ali nervous. Laird complained to me that Raymond should have spoken to him because he had been helping Martin. That he had been working on something with Fresh Start's mental health guys. And what were you working on, Laird? I didn't wait for an answer because he and I both knew he didn't have one to give. But he had one more curveball to throw.

What are you going to do now?

What do you mean?

How's he going to handle all that money by himself? Did you ever think of that?

The bastard had a point. Once Martin cashed his check, Big Pete and every dope fiend in the city would be on him like white on rice and that twenty-one K would be gone, man, gone. They'd beat his ass, take his money, and leave him bloody and broke if not dead.

But Martin wanted his money. He might have been crazy

as a crack whore, but he wasn't so far gone he didn't know he had been approved for disability. And Laird kept tweaking him: Where's your money, Martin? Where's your money?

Raymond had given the disability people the shelter as Martin's address. He locked the big check and the monthly checks that followed in a safe and put Martin off when he asked about them by giving him a few bucks out of pocket. But Laird wouldn't let up. He would buy Martin breakfast and ask him why he hadn't received his money.

The checks started piling up. Laird took Martin to the disability office to complain. The disability people called and asked why we weren't giving him his money. I told Raymond this couldn't continue.

Raymond said he would get Martin a bank account so he could deposit his money and save it. I said, Yeah? Martin's going to walk into a bank and set up a savings account? I'll go with him, Raymond said. What's to stop him from withdrawing all of it at once? I said. I'll make it a joint account, Raymond said. He can't withdraw anything without my signature.

I'd had other staff, formerly homeless guys like Laird, get the good Samaritan bug and try to help some of our other head cases with their money by managing it for them. But each time the money got the best of them. They'd take a bit here, a bit there. They'd start getting high again. Finally, they'd disappear and the money with them, leaving the head case howling at the moon.

If I let Raymond help Martin start a bank account, the rest of the staff would want to know why I wouldn't let them do the same thing for the many other Martins we had. They'd have all these dollar signs dancing in their eyes and accuse me of letting Raymond get over with Martin. I'd have a small riot on my hands.

No way, I told Raymond, and explained why.

Wait, he said. I know someone who could do it for me. A bank teller. He goes to my church.

Sometimes I envied Raymond his faith. How he could read passages from the Bible and believe without question. If you ask me what I believe, I couldn't tell you. Surviving, I guess. Not giving a shit. I wonder when I first walked around someone passed out on the sidewalk and did not think: I just walked past a body on the sidewalk. When I first got into social services, I used to check to see if they were breathing. A few times, they weren't. I called 911 and waited around for the police or the ambulance. And whoever showed up first would always ask at some point, Why'd you check to see if they were breathing? As if that was the strangest thing to do. And maybe I finally agreed that it was. I don't know. I stopped doing it after a while though. I mean, they were dead. It was a little late to see if they were breathing.

After I give Big Pete my change, I keep walking to the admin building, passing the convenience store on the corner of Turk and Leavenworth where guys deal crack and stray dogs nuzzle through trash and get kicked in the ass. I push the buzzer, say who I am, and listen for the door to unlock. I jog up a flight of stairs to McGraw's office and knock on his door. It swings open and I see him hunched in front of his computer half reading aloud from a budget spreadsheet. He has on a suit and one of those thin leather ties I see billboard models wearing. He's going bald and shaves his head, and the ceiling light's reflection shines his scalp. McGraw adjusts his glasses and scrolls down to a column of numbers. Then he swivels around in his chair, careful not to spill files stacked ankle high around his feet, and faces me.

What's up?

You have a minute? I ask.

Sure, he says. I wanted to talk to you anyway.

There's a problem with Raymond and a client.

I know. Laird told me about it. That's why I wanted to speak to you. What's going on?

Yeah, I saw Laird on the way over.

McGraw looks back at his computer and smiles.

We're doing really, really well, he says pointing at the spreadsheet. Too well. We're under budget. We have to start spending more, otherwise the mayor's office will reduce our city contracts next year.

McGraw stretches his arms and cracks his knuckles. He takes off his glasses and rubs them against his jacket. A few months back, he had me tell the different program directors to reduce spending so we'd make it to the end of the year in the black. I guess everyone cut back too much. Now, we have the reverse problem. Not much of a problem though. I can see McGraw's already thinking how to spend the extra cash. A new computer maybe? I clear my throat. McGraw glances at me again with this oh-damn-forgot-you-were-here expression.

About Raymond, I say.

Right. Like I said, Laird came by and said Raymond lost someone's money?

Yeah, Raymond just told me. That's why I came to see you. It's serious.

McGraw spins around and faces the computer, begins scrolling columns of numbers. He really doesn't want to deal with me.

How serious?

Well, I say, Raymond helped this client by getting him on disability. And then he got him a bank account and set him up with a guy to manage his money. And the guy screwed up somehow.

Who's this guy?

A bank teller. I had told Raymond we can't handle a client's money. And I thought that was that. But without telling me, Raymond goes and asks this guy he knew, this bank teller who attends Raymond's church, to handle the client's money. To be the cosigner, you know, on the bank account so the client couldn't take out all his money and blow it without the teller signing off on it.

McGraw sighs and turns back to face me again. All he wants is for me to go away so he can stare at his good numbers. I can hear him mumbling, trying to figure out how he can move money from this line item to that line item. Especially if he can slip more money into admin. Line up some salary bonuses for management maybe. Raymond's an unwanted interruption.

And then what? McGraw says.

Well, according to Raymond, it was going good for a couple of months. But then the teller got laid off. His last week on the job, the client comes in for some money. He signs the withdrawal slip, the teller fills out the rest like he always had. But this time he put in for all the money and closed the account. He gave the client his little bit of cash and kept the rest. In other words, he basically took all the money and split. Raymond hasn't seen or heard from him since.

McGraw rests his chin in his hands and sucks in a deep breath. You're saying the bank teller stole the client's money?

Yes, except for the little bit he gave the client. The teller just lost his job. I think he saw this as a chance to have a cash cushion.

When'd you know about this?

Today, I say, looking right at McGraw and willing myself not to blink. Just now.

Laird seemed to think you knew all about it from the start.

I didn't, I say. You know how Laird is. Always looking for somebody to point the finger at.

McGraw cleans a thumbnail with a pen cap.

Yeah, that's Laird, he says. If it's a cloudy day he blames us. OK, what do we do about this?

I know what I have to say but choke on it and cough. I wipe my mouth, try to get rid of the bad taste on my tongue. I can't even swallow. Just say it, I think. It's the only way. Sorry, Raymond.

We fire Raymond, I say, speaking a little too fast.

Of course we fire Raymond, McGraw says. But what about the money that's missing? I don't like it, but we're going to have to pay it back. How much we talking about?

I hesitate again. I'm not about to say, You know, McGraw, you're right. We got to pay Martin back. But all that extra money you think you have? You don't because we owe Martin twenty-odd grand.

McGraw would have to tell his board of directors. The mayor's office would demand an investigation. Our city contract renewals would be fucked. I'd be out of a job so fast the door wouldn't have time to slam my ass on the way out.

I tell McGraw: The client's owed like five hundred dollars or something, but we don't pay a thing. Raymond does. We tell him to sign over his last payroll check to the client. It will cover what was lost and then some. Raymond can keep the change. As part of the deal, we'll call his firing a layoff. Raymond can get unemployment that way. He can use us as a reference. He'll agree. He won't have a choice, and we'll stay out of it.

McGraw nods, picks at his chin. I don't move. As long as Martin gets a disability check each month, he won't understand how much is missing.

All right, McGraw says. Write this all up and fire Raymond. Lay him off I mean. I'll have the fiscal department draft a statement for him to sign agreeing to turn over his check to the client. Anything else?

No, everything else is fine.

We have to be careful who we hire, McGraw says. I'm sure

Raymond had good intentions, but we want people who know when to leave their good intentions at the door. We don't have expectations. We're not trying to save lives. Just trying to make them a little better.

Right, I say.

He turns back to his computer. I leave his office and am out in the hall when McGraw calls me back.

Put out a memo for me, he says. Tell the program directors we're under budget. Tell them to think of some things they need and how they'd like to spend the money. Bus tokens. Anything we can blow it on and get away with. And we got some people coming by next week from the Bank of America Foundation. Let me know who you'll set me up with, who our success stories are this month.

Outside the admin building, I rest my hands on my knees and take a deep breath. My body feels strange to me, as if it's no longer mine. I look around with a feeling of total detachment as though I'm seeing the TL for the first time, hovering between the street and the sky in a low-flying plane.

I think about what I'll tell Raymond. I smell the stink where people have pissed on the sidewalk, cover my nose, and head to the shelter. McGraw was much easier than I expected. Too easy. I mean, really, I was nervous at first but then it was nothing not to tell him about the twenty-one grand. To say that Raymond's check would cover everything.

What bullshit, but it's what McGraw wanted to hear. Like the Bank of America types coming next week, these people who give money to Fresh Start. Sometimes they call and ask to see the shelter and drop-in, especially around Christmas. The day before they show up, I run around and get the staff to mop and clean the place. Then I go to thrift stores to buy clothes for the people we want to pass off as success stories. The guys who have some sort of job history, who don't get hammered every damn day and who are pretty reliable volunteers. Guys who have all their teeth and their fingers aren't stained with tobacco tar. Guys who look pretty much like anyone else.

I give McGraw their names and he introduces them to the funders like they're his personal friends. Here's Richard or Terry or Mick. He's in our jobs program. And as Richard or Terry or Mick works with our jobs counselor, he also volunteers in our maintenance department to develop skills he can put on a résumé. We believe in self-help, McGraw will say.

Richard or Terry or Mick is a good homeless person. Soon he will rejoin the nuclear family. The funders smile and leave satisfied. They are good people too for helping out a place like Fresh Start. They'll come by again next year and get their ticket to heaven punched once more.

After they leave, I'll give Richard or Terry or Mick a few bucks so they can buy some booze or score some dope and calm their nerves after talking to suits for an hour. Just be here again next week, I'll tell them. We got some more people coming by.

As Raymond would say: He who chases fantasies lacks judgment. I mean, really. After a while, it gets so way past sickening that I no longer feel disgust. I don't. I just keep telling everybody what they want to hear.

Just before I go into the shelter, I get this uneasy feeling. Laird won't shut up with Raymond gone. He'll keep talking shit and saying how I knew from jump street what was going on with Martin's money until something else comes along that he can bitch about. But when will that be? He knows we owe Martin a shitload of money. I stop walking. He knows. He'll ask Martin if we paid him back. He'll ask how much we've given him. Martin will tell him. Laird will ask more questions. He'll figure it out. That we haven't even come close to paying Martin twenty-one K.

Raymond is sitting at his desk reading his Bible. He looks up at me and says, In my trouble I cried to the Lord, and He answered me.

What's that from?

Psalms. Chapter 120, verse 1.

Close the Bible, Raymond.

He leans forward, leaves the Bible open.

I know, he says.

I'm sorry, I say. I tried.

Thank you.

McGraw wants you to sign your check over to Martin. To make up for some of the money you lost. Fiscal's going to write something up and then you sign it and then Fresh Start will cut your last check to Martin.

I'll do that, Raymond says without looking up. What about you?

What about me?

What did McGraw do to you?

I've been suspended without pay for a few days.

I'm sorry.

It's nothing compared to you.

Raymond looks down. I don't know if he's reading the Bible again or just staring at the floor praying. I'm talking to him like I rehearsed the words from a script. The secret to lying is that you have to believe what you're saying so you don't even know you're lying. You become someone else. This isn't me talking. I'm reciting someone else's lines.

What about the rest of it?

The rest of what?

Martin's money?

McGraw says we'll cover that, I say.

Raymond looks up. I hold his stare.

You should go by the end of the day, Raymond. I'll tell the staff. McGraw's calling this a layoff. You'll be eligible for unemployment. We'll give you a reference. He's giving you a break. He doesn't want an honest mistake to dog you.

Raymond nods, closes the Bible. He puts it in a small leather case and zips it shut. He takes down his university degree from the wall. He looks around his desk as if he should have more things to take with him, but there's nothing else other than sign-in sheets, referrals, and a box of bus tokens.

I'm going to keep up with Martin, Raymond says. He needs someone to help him. I'll set up another bank account for him. I'll manage it this time.

But Raymond, I begin.

He holds up a finger, silences me.

The Christian who is pure and without fault, from God the Father's point of view, is the one who takes care of orphans and widows, and who remains true to the Lord—not soiled and dirtied by his contacts with the world. James, chapter 1, verse 27. I want you to call me when Martin gets his check from McGraw.

I don't miss a beat.

Sure, Raymond, I say. I'll do that.

I go back outside. I stare down at my shoes, my mind a blank for a hot minute before it gets all kinds of crazy with thoughts about Laird and Raymond and how I'm going to handle them. More rats race along the curb into a sewer. My skin crawls. Jesus, they make me feel dirty. I press my hands against my ears, try to keep my mind from racing. Slow down, I tell myself, slow down, but I can't. I hadn't thought through on Laird and I hadn't expected Raymond would want to keep up with Martin. I mean, he just lost his job and all he thinks about is Martin. No, I hadn't seen that one coming at all.

I look around and try to shake this sense of doom settling

on me, but my head feels all stuffed, like it's about to explode. I see Big Pete across the street with Ross and John still hustling outside the drop-in. Man, to think they had apartments in the Richmond at one time. Now nothing, their faces dirt-streaked and wide-eyed jittery, and their clothes smelling of damp nights spent in Golden Gate Park.

Pete notices me and lifts his chin.

I put up my hands like I'm out of change and shrug.

He laughs. I keep looking at him and just like that I know what I need to do. My head clears. Come here, Pete, I think. He stares back and stops laughing. My eyes don't budge off his. There's this invisible line between us drawing him to me. Come here, Pete. He walks across the street under my spell.

What? he says.

You hear about Laird?

Laird? What about him?

He came into some money. I'm talking a lot. Inheritance, I think.

Laird?

Twenty-one grand, man. Twenty-one and then some grand. He's fat, I'm telling you.

Laird? Twenty-one grand? Bullshit.

He's got it on him. Showed me the check this morning. He's showing everybody. You know how Laird is.

I watch the reflection of my face swell and shrink in Pete's sunglasses.

Yeah, I know how Laird is.

Twenty-some-odd grand, I'm telling you Pete.

You for real?

Serious as a heart attack, Pete.

What's it matter? Why're you telling me this?

I want Laird to pick up the slack. I'm tired of giving you all my money.

Pete forces out a half laugh but he's not smiling. He doesn't take his eyes off me. His raw smoker's breath jet-fueled by the funk of his coat stifles my face. Not doing his little speed freak bopping moves. Not doing anything but trying to slow his nerves down enough to think from A to B to C. He knows if he rolls Laird, he can go to any check-cashing place and get money.

Pete turns away and goes to cross the street but hangs back a little, head down like he's concentrating on his shoes. Ross and John watch him, know something's up. Pigeons rise from the sidewalk toward what little sunlight is beginning to penetrate the fog. The noise they make crashes down on my head like unfurling rolls of carpet. I don't move.

I can't say if Pete will bite or not, but he's sure thinking about it. Check-cashing places don't require ID. They take a 20 percent cut, no questions asked. Pete's doing the math. He doesn't have to be a rocket scientist to figure it out. He knows he would have seventeen thousand dollars and some change in his pocket just like that.

I think it's a good bet he'll roll Laird for his check. Except there won't be a check. I don't know what I'll do when Pete, Ross, and John beat the crap out of Laird and then realize he doesn't have a dime on him.

I do know that Laird'll be laid up and in too much pain to do any talking about us owing Martin more money than we paid him. And Raymond? If he really does help Martin get another bank account and then finds out that there's no check coming from McGraw?

Well, that'll be a problem too. It definitely will.

I'll tell him something.

Katie

Her name was Gloria Gonzalez, but we always called her Mrs. G, although I'm sure she wouldn't have minded if we'd called her Gloria. She owned La Taqueria, a Mexican restaurant up the street from Fresh Start. There was something about her—her thick white hair; her stooped shoulders, and the grooved worry lines in her face; the determined way she moved from table to table, wiping them clean, adjusting the plastic tablecloths; how she stood alone in the kitchen over the food-spattered stove, sweating, stirring pots of beans and rice, warming tortillas wrapped in tinfoil one by one—that gave me the impression of someone who had worked hard for years and had grown old because of it, unlike most of us who had aged by wasting our lives drinking. And because of that, I think we all thought she deserved nothing less than the respect of being called Mrs. G, someone who had taken life on and done something with it instead of hiding behind a bottle. But some people, like Hank, played her. Not because he disrespected her. Just the opposite. He liked her. But he was an alcoholic. He wasn't drinking then, but he still thought in a street way. I'm not judging him. My sponsor, Stacey, would've jumped me for doing anything close to that. I'm just saying that one thing leads to another is how I see it, and eventually it did.

Mrs. G had a smile that filled her face, but she had a sad look about her too, which told us, or at least me, that she'd lost people in her life. I understood that. When I sobered up and began working the steps, the hardest one I had to deal with was the fourth, the one where you make amends. I wanted to apologize to my mom and dad for my drinking, but they had passed before I cleaned up. When I first got sober, Stacey suggested I write letters to them and then burn the letters and watch the ashes float into the air rising to heaven, a symbolic way of reaching them and others I'd hurt and who were no longer here. I looked at her like she was nuts. Symbolism is sort of horseshit, she admitted, but sometimes horseshit works.

I wrote the letters. It was hard. I tried to explain why I did what I did when I'd been drinking, what was going on in my head, but after a while I realized there was no way to explain it other than I'm an alcoholic and will always be one, except now, unlike then, I'm not drinking—one day at a time. I'm sorry for all the ways I hurt you, I wrote to each of them, I mean it. Love, Katie. I hoped that was enough. Sometimes less is more, Stacey told me. We were sitting in the backyard of her house with glasses of Coke. I held the letters over a grill and lit them with a lighter. The edges of the paper turned orange, curling into black ash. Thin white smoke rose and disappeared. I started crying, feeling the absence of my folks, my body clean of booze but my heart filled with this ache of missing them. I'm sorry, I said, again and again. Stacey held me, and I wanted to believe that she was my mom and dad and a whole bunch of other people I'd hurt, all of them hugging on me, but I could only take this symbolic crap so far. It was just Stacey, and I was grateful but it wasn't near enough. She couldn't make up for all of them who were gone and owed an apology. Maybe that was a good thing. Maybe they wouldn't have accepted my apology. Hank told me when he tried to apologize to his family, his stepdad slammed the door in his face. If my real dad had been around it would have been different, he said, but he left when I was a kid.

I don't know about that, any more than I know if people go to heaven or hell. I hope my folks went to heaven and saw the smoke from the letters and know how sorry I am. Not that they were saints. They drank and owe me more than a few amends, but they aren't here and I am. They can't write letters where they're at, Stacey reminded me. She was right. I stopped drinking, they didn't, and I'm alive so it was on me to apologize, and I'm glad I did but I feel incomplete. Like there's more to be said. Like I need to hear something from them even though I know I can't. The Big Book talks about humility. Be mad and keep drinking, or be humble and let things go and stay sober. We all have to learn to forgive people who never tell us they're sorry, Stacey told me. No one said it'd be easy.

I think Mrs. G understood me, like she knew I carried the same kind of sadness she did. I'd come into her place for lunch and she'd pat me on the shoulder and with that tired smile of hers she'd say, La vida mejorará, Katie, and then she'd repeat it in English: Life will get better, Katie. I always picked a corner table across from a painting of a ship on the ocean under a clear sky. Sailfish jumped out of the water and people on the boat faced them. I wondered where the ship was and where it might be headed.

Mrs. G opened La Taqueria about a year or so ago. Before she moved in, it had been a fast-food burger joint and before that a coffee and doughnut shop. Those places closed because too often the owners extended credit to formerly homeless people, recovering addicts like me, who worked at one of the social services agencies around here, including Fresh Start, assuming, I guess, that since they had jobs, they'd be good for it, but many weren't. Too many. An addict with credit, even one who is in recovery but still thinks in the street way, doesn't look at it like they owe money. Instead, they feel they got a break, conned the system, and have money to spend on something else and maybe get that on credit too.

I remember Mr. Papier, the owner of the burger place, coming into Fresh Start and speaking to Tom about the money owed to him by some of the staff. I could tell this kind of BS beat Tom down. He told everyone to pay their bills. Some of them did but most didn't, and Tom couldn't make them. It was between them and Mr. Papier. Eventually, Mr. Papier shut down just like the coffee and doughnut shop had. I can't say he closed because staff at Fresh Start and the other agencies didn't pay their bills, but it didn't help, I'm sure.

I never fell into the credit trap. I know me. I don't even have an ATM card. I'm a cash-only kind of gal. I don't owe anyone. It's a hassle going to the bank to withdraw money so I don't spend much of what I take out, which is a good thing because I don't have much to spend. It's not like I earn a fortune at Fresh Start. But once, twice a week I'd go to Mrs. G's as a treat to myself. It got so she knew what I wanted without me having to say anything. Chicken taco plate? she'd say to me when I walked in. You got it, I'd say. She'd carry it out on a big platter and warn me that it was very hot. It smelled all kinds of good, and I'd poke at the refried beans and yellow rice with a fork to let the heat out of it. If it was a slow day, Mrs. G would sit with me and tell me about her childhood in Puerto Rico. She'd spread her arms to show me how big the palm trees were and how she learned to crack open coconuts as a little girl and drink the milk inside. She said the ocean was so clear you could see all sorts of fish—just like in that painting I liked, and she'd point to it—and chickens would roam the beach and she'd chase them with her friends. When she went back into the kitchen, I'd look at the painting and imagine her looking at the water or running on the beach after chickens, and then I'd try to see myself and I'd laugh at the idea of me trying to catch chickens.

I warned Mrs. G not to give credit to anyone at Fresh Start when she first opened, and she didn't. Then some of her Fresh Start regulars whined about being broke, and she'd feel bad for them. That's how it started. She told me when she was growing up no one had much money and everybody helped each other, and I think she kind of looked at her customers the same way, as neighbors in need. Give it to me tomorrow, Mrs. G would say, and tomorrow would come and they wouldn't have it. Give it to me tomorrow, she'd say again, and the next day they'd come up with another excuse and she'd give them another break until she was in it so deep it was like, You already owe me so much, what's another ten dollars? I think she got caught up in her own screwy thinking.

When it came to not paying, Hank was one of the worst. He owed Mrs. G I don't know how much. He was smooth. Oh, Mrs. G, can you give me a burrito just this once? I haven't eaten all day. I promise I'll pay my bill tomorrow, and she'd give him this look like she knew it was a lie, but she'd give it to him. Hank had it going on with her because he could make her laugh. She was married, her husband worked with her sometimes, but he had his own little lawn business and wasn't around much. Hank didn't care. He flirted with her, husband or no husband, and some of the things he'd say would make her blush red as a tomato. You know Mrs. G, he told her one afternoon, it ain't the size of the spoon but how you stir the batter, and he faced her and swiveled his hips in front of everyone in there and then he stepped around the counter and into the kitchen and kissed her on the cheek. I swear she was like a teenager, she got so flustered.

His charm didn't linger once he left. Mrs. G would complain to me about him and I'd tell her I was so sorry he was doing her like he was, but she had to quit being so nice to him. Then I'd get on him about his bill. You gotta pay the woman, I told him. I'm tired of apologizing for you. Don't worry about it, Katie, he'd say. I'll handle it. But he never did. He shouldn't have even been here. He'd left Fresh Start for a job at Walmart but he didn't last long and Tom hired him back. He said he hadn't fit in at Walmart. His coworkers would invite him to a bar after work and he'd have to explain that he didn't drink. They'd ask him where he had worked before, and he'd tell them about Fresh Start and how it was the only steady job he'd had in years, because he had been homeless for so long. He said it was like telling people he had cancer. No one knew what to say to him.

Hank continued to charm Mrs. G out of food until the day he started drinking again. I hadn't seen his slip coming. He didn't show up for his shift one morning, but I thought he was just late. Then he called me, sounding all out of breath, almost like he was frightened. He asked me to meet him at Leavenworth and O'Farrell streets. I didn't know what to think, so I rushed up there. On my way, I saw Mrs. G unlocking the door to her restaurant and I raised a hand but she didn't see me. Then I saw Walter, sitting on a milk crate outside a convenience store with a bottle, and he asked me to put him in detox. You know where to go, I told him. How about a dollar, Katie? I shook my head. I thought of that painting at Mrs. G's and how I'd like to take a trip one day just to be in a place where no one knew me.

I found Hank standing by a bus shelter across from a liquor store. I didn't remember it from my drinking days and that bothered me. So much of my memory is shot, my life lost to so many blackouts that I can't even remember a liquor store I'm sure I used. That's saying something. But maybe I never did buy booze at this store.

Katie, Hank said.

Hi, Hank.

There was none of his usual shuck and jive. He gave me this look that said, I fucked up, but I knew that right off, look or no look. The neck of a pint bottle of whiskey stuck out of his jacket pocket. He wore blue jeans and white sneakers. His shirt looked crooked, like he had buttoned it wrong. I noticed dried mud on one side of his face and a cut on his left ear.

I don't know why I called you. I'm just so mad, Katie. I'm just so mad.

About what? What happened?

He spit on the sidewalk.

What happened, Hank? I asked again.

He looked at me, his bloodshot eyes carrying a kind of hurt that I'd not seen in him before but felt within myself more than a few times back in the day, all sorts of torments I wouldn't speak of and would use as excuses to drink.

I just get so frustrated sometimes, Katie.

He wrung his hands. He sat down in the shelter, dropped his head and stared, then started crying.

It's OK, Hank, I tell him. We'll talk about this later. For now, let's go to detox.

It was *me* who put *you* in detox.

I know. This is payback.

He gave me a half smile, wiped his eyes.

That's a good one, Katie. Remember when I said if I ever started drinking again, I'd never go to Fresh Start to detox, because it would be too embarrassing?

Yeah, and I said that kind of thinking is a good way to keep on drinking.

Yeah. When was that?

I don't know, Hank. A while.

He stood and wiped his eyes again.

I'm going to go. I'll be all right, Katie, he said.

No, you won't. Not like this.

I better go.

He gave me a sloppy hug, stumbling, grinding his crotch against me as I tried to keep my balance.

Stop it! I said and slapped his shoulder.

He laughed.

Thank you, Katie.

Come with me to detox.

No, I'd better just go.

Hank.

He put a finger to his lips and shook his head.

Call me, I told him.

He walked off stiff-legged. I hoped he might turn around but he didn't. I watched him until I couldn't see him anymore and then I walked back to work, past Walter, again nodding out. Mrs. G stood in the door of La Taqueria and waved me over, asked me if I'd seen Hank.

I'm sorry, Mrs. G, I said. I don't know where he is.

Tom helped Mrs. G collect most of what the staff owed her. He even paid off Hank's bill. In return, he made her promise to stop extending credit. I continued having my taco plate twice a week. Then without notice she shut down. One day she was open, the next day a For Rent sign hung in the window. I don't know where she went. It hurt that she had said nothing to me about closing. We weren't friends exactly, but we had an under-standing, at least I thought we did. I hope she landed on her feet. I hope she opened a new restaurant in a neighborhood where normal people eat. I haven't seen Hank. He might have gone south to San Jose and gotten into an alcohol program down there. I hope so.

Sometimes, I think of that painting in La Taqueria. When I do, I can almost smell the food and Mrs. G's warm touch on my shoulder. I hope a new restaurant opens. I don't need to know the owner. I just want a place I can go, eat, and leave without drama. I'm sorry for enough things in my own life. I don't need to apologize for what other people do.

Walter

This guy's looking down at me. I'm on the ground, against a tree in Golden Gate Park, and he just stands there staring. A band's playing. There's kind of like a festival going on, I guess. This is the third band up since I got here, I don't know, maybe two hours ago. Has sort of a country vibe going.

The grass smells sharp and sweet like it's just been cut. There's a fresh and gentle breeze carrying salt air from the Bay. Couples sit on blankets with Tupperware and plastic forks and spoons and bottles of wine. I snatched one when this guy and this gal weren't looking. They were dancing and I picked it up off their blanket. Really they were more like swaying, arms out, barefoot, faces turned to the sky, eyes closed. Maybe they're a little tight and that's why they're dancing. I understand that. I don't dance unless I'm drunk. Whatever. They didn't see me and still don't know that anything's missing. They're still listening to the music, their backs to me. Other people stand and sway to the rhythm. Young colts and old fucks like me. A warm day, all shorts and crop tops, and dudes bare-chested.

I remember working construction one summer as a kid, teenager really. Pushing wheelbarrows filled with concrete, laying tar paper, the sun above us, our bodies sucking in the heat. My skin turned to bronze. I walked home draping my T-shirt around my neck, a sweat-soaked scarf. Girls in halter tops and short shorts walking past, do a double take, dragging their cunts on the sidewalk for me, I knew. I felt my power. Went to The Spot, ordered a pitcher of beer I drank by myself. I got drunk with friends one night and bit my glass, breaking it. I spit the broken pieces out of my mouth, laughed, wiped my cut lips with the back of my hand.

Have I seen you before? the guy goes.

I squint up at him, raise my chin.

Huh?

Have I seen you before?

I don't know. Maybe. Why? What do you want?

The guy shrugs, shakes his head. Nothing.

He's got on a wrinkled button-down shirt that's a little large for him and blue jeans, also too big. Thrift store clothes or some agency's donation closet, I'm thinking. That kind of stuff never fits right. That kind of need isn't too particular either. His wet hair dampens his shoulders. I don't know him, don't think so anyway.

At Fresh Start, he says. You were in detox. I was in the bed next to you.

I turn to the band. An older woman's singing a John Prine tune, "Angel from Montgomery." I'm trying to think, When was I in detox? Four days ago, maybe. I had pneumonia. I didn't know it then, but I was coughing so much that Katie sent me to General the next morning and the doctors there kept me for a minute. I was in a bed with beeping machines on either side, and I had an IV in my left arm filling me with antibiotics and valium too, so I could ease off the booze without major withdrawal. It was a nice feeling, a different kind of buzz, I got to say, smooth and nice like the colors of a fall day when you first wake up and feel the cool dawn air, and it lifted me and I felt myself sailing through air, more like floating, really, no speed to it at all, and I thought of my mom's driveway and the heavy branches

200

of elms that stretched over it and the shadows and squirrels in the shadows and how I came home from that construction job, the squirrels running, and my mother said, Put your shirt on. You look like a common laborer, and the girls cruising past as I tugged it back on, felt it stick to my sweating arms, cling to my chest, cicadas buzzing through the humidity.

I don't remember you, I tell the guy.

Yeah, it was you next to me. You were sick. You left in the morning, I think.

I look at him.

Sounds like me.

He nods. It doesn't matter to him if I remember. He keeps talking anyway.

I needed shelter. I'd been sleeping in my car and wanted a break. There was this social worker, I forget his name.

Oscar, I say.

Yeah, that's right. That's his name. He said the shelter was full but he could get me into detox. Are you an alcoholic? he goes, and I go, No, and he goes, Listen to me. The shelter is full but I can get you into detox if you're an alcoholic, understand? So I'm going to ask you again. Are you an alcoholic? I didn't even know what detox was, man. Hell, I'd never heard of Fresh Start. A cop made me move my car that morning and told me about it. Anyway, I got it, you know what I'm saying? I got Oscar's drift, so I said, Yes, I'm an alcoholic, and he put me in detox.

Oscar always has his game on.

I suppose, the guy says.

I close my eyes. My chest still hurts from the pneumonia every time I take a deep breath. The woman has stopped singing. A guitar player strums something low and slow, kind of twangy. A harmonica kicks in. The sun warms my face. Before I was discharged from General, the social worker gave me a two-week referral to the Apollo, one of the shittier welfare hotels on Sixth Street. She also found some clean clothes—a 49ers T-shirt, blue jeans, and white socks. I took off my hospital gown, dressed, wondered who the clothes had belonged to—who died and left me their rags? Would somebody see me in the dead guy's clothes and think I'm him? Would he be alive again for just that moment? Oh, sorry, I thought you were somebody else, I can hear someone saying to me. The social worker told me not to think like that. But I do. I think that way about myself in my room at the Apollo with just my radio and a *Penthouse* magazine I found. How many dead guys have worn these clothes? No one knows, I'm sure. I feel bad for them. Not bad, I guess, just weird. Like putting on someone else's skin. I'll be one of them: dead someday. I've been wearing these duds now for three days. They got my stink. Whoever wore them before is totally gone. They're fucking mine now. I could use a comb. Some deodorant and toothpaste too.

The woman starts singing again. I don't recognize the song. I didn't know there'd be music. I just wanted out of the Apollo. There are so many rats on the sill I won't open the windows. The hall shower doesn't work and the cracked sink in my room sags off the wall, leaking. Cockroaches converge at night on the brown carpet. Rice Krispies, I say when I step on them. I stay up nights and sleep in the day, avoiding the funk of my room behind closed eyes. I turn the radio on at night for the company of better-off voices. This morning, that wasn't enough. I needed real people, people I could see, so I caught the Muni for the Haight, got off at Masonic and walked to the park.

How long were you in detox? I ask the guy.

I'm still there, he says. They're letting me stay till next week when I go into a forty-five-day recovery program. I don't need it. I'm not a drunk, but they say that after you complete it they'll send you to a halfway house and help you find a job. So I'm thinking, Why not? That Oscar guy gave me a day pass today because I've been going a little crazy sitting around Fresh Start.

I hear you. You want a drink?

No, man. Shit, what did I just say? I can't go back with booze on my breath. They'd throw me out and that'd be that.

You said you're not an alcoholic.

I'm not.

One drink won't fuck up your breath.

Sure it will. I'm no drunk but I've had a few drinks in my time. I know.

I bet. He doesn't say anything more but he's thinking about it, I can see it in his face. That look that says he's getting a contact high just talking about drinking. I got the bottle I stole behind me. I feel it against the small of my back. The couple's still dancing, the sun beating down on them, their long hair sticking to their necks. I remember this woman I met in a bar, The Déjà Vu, in my construction days. She worked at a Pizza Hut and asked me to dance. It was a slow number. A mirror ball turned slowly above our heads, all sorts of colored lights spinning on the floor and covering our bodies with thin hues of pink and purple and green that barely penetrated the dark. I held her, felt her tits on my chest, her waist against my belt buckle, the feel of her back against the palm of my hand. The press of her against me.

Well, if you change your mind, I say, and lean to one side and show him the bottle.

No thanks.

OK. You can sit down.

I don't know.

OK.

I'm not drinking.

203

You can sit. No one will smell sitting on your breath.

He gives me a smirk, lowers himself to the ground, and crosses his legs. The band stops playing and exits the platform. I watch the couple return to their blanket. They don't seem to notice the missing wine. She unzips a shoulder pack and takes out two plastic bags with sandwiches, and then she works her hand around inside it and removes a bag full of grapes. After handing the guy a sandwich, she takes out two glasses, looks left and right, and frowns. She says something to him and they get up and turn in circles, staring down at the blanket. OK, they've noticed now. I don't want them to see me watching them, so I stop staring. I can't resist though, and after a second or two I shoot a sidelong glance in their direction. Looks like they're arguing, probably blaming each other for forgetting the wine. I feel sort of bad about that, but not too bad.

You sure you don't want a drink?

I wouldn't mind one, but what've I been telling you? I can't.

More for me.

The guy smiles.

You know what they say.

What? the guy asks.

I don't know. They say a lot of things.

He laughed.

You're crazy.

Yeah, maybe.

I really want to get to work again, he says. I had a maintenance job at a country club in Walnut Creek, but I got laid off. I've been driving for Uber and Lyft but that doesn't pay the bills. So I gave up my apartment and started staying in my car. I got to tell you when they put me in detox and I laid out in a real bed after weeks in my car—well, it was a cot, but you know what I'm saying—and I could stretch my legs, oh, man, did it feel good.

What kind of car?

Honda Civic.

Little thing.

Tell me about it.

I'm going to drink.

Do your thing, bro.

I reach behind me for the bottle. A new band has come on. A man growls out the Johnny Cash tune "Folsom Prison Blues." The couple lean against each other like nothing else matters. That's nice, I think. Good for them. It's only a bottle of wine. I don't feel anything about taking their wine now. Everything's worked out. They can get another one without thinking. I can't. The guy with me watches the couple too. Or maybe he's just looking in their direction; I don't know what's going on in his head. That Pizza Hut gal kissed me on the cheek when we stopped dancing. Thank you, she said and went back to her table and the girls with her. I stood like a dumbass in the middle of the floor beneath the disco ball. I should've gone after her, but I wasn't drunk enough to hit on her. By the time I was, she was gone. I wonder what would have happened if she and I had dated. I'd've taken her to a movie and a restaurant and shit like that. I'd've fucked with her, absolutely, but there'd be nights I'd sneak off to the bars. I was a drinker even then. I can hear the arguments we'd've had. I had them with other girlfriends. I'd've fucked it up like I did with them.

What you got there? the guy asks me.

I look at the wine label on the bottle.

Zinfandel, red.

You got the good shit.

Yeah.

No Thunderbird for you.

You know Thunderbird?

Oh, yeah. Those nights in my car, yeah. You hit the lottery.

Just got lucky.

It's a corked bottle, not a twist-off. Like the guy said, this is the good shit. Searching the ground, I take a stick and press it against the cork inching it down until it drops into the bottle spurting wine. I scooch back to avoid the geyser. Raising the bottle to my mouth, I drink, spit out bits of cork. Sweet, but not as sweet as Thunderbird. That's pure sugar compared to this. I take another hit. A warmth spreads through my body, rises to my head, expanding before it settles like a quilt and fills me with quiet. I close my eyes. This is what love feels like, I think, sinking deep into it. After a moment, I let out a deep breath, cringe at the pain in my chest. That brings me back. I open my eyes and raise the bottle toward the guy.

You sure?

He shakes his head.

All yours.

C'mon, man. One swallow. Won't kill you. When do you have to be back?

Five.

Plenty of time. Get something to eat and you'll be fine.

With what money? he asks.

Dumpster dive, I say.

No way am I digging in trash for food. I'm not there yet. They'll have some soup in detox.

I hold the bottle out to him. He stares at it, shakes his head again.

C'mon.

What do you care? Do you want to fuck things up for me?

I take a swallow.

No. I'm just in a sociable mood.

Have you been in a program?

I have, I say, lowering the bottle.

What do you do in them? I mean, how do they work? I guess if they figure out I'm not a drunk they'll just kick me out, right? And I'll be back in my car. But I really want a halfway house and a job.

Listen, I tell him. You just sit around and go to AA meetings and talk about your emotions and stuff and how to deal with shit without drinking. You admit alcohol calls all the shots in your life, and you promise to swear off it a day at a time. They'll talk about a higher power. Go all in on that. When they ask you stuff, just talk about times you've been drunk and make it sound like it was a daily thing. Don't trip. It's easy.

Do you know the one in Redwood City?

I was there. It's nice. Lots of woods around it. Guys only. That's kind of a drag. But all in all, it's not bad. Good food.

Let's see. I was at Redwood a year ago, maybe a little more. I graduated and got into Hospital Center, a halfway house in the Mission. I was doing good for almost two, no, three weeks. Yeah, three, and it was the strangest thing that happened that fucked things up. I'm out and about one afternoon, had gone by Fresh Start to show Katie how good I was doing, and then I left to go back to the Mission. I got to the corner of Van Ness and Golden Gate to catch a bus when I heard, Stop him! and this dude ran past me shoving people out of his way and tossing a purse I guess he'd snatched. Everyone kind of pulled back like, What the fuck? and he just barreled through us and then all these people chased after him. They crossed an intersection, stoplight flashing DON'T WALK, and knocked down a woman in a purple dress, and her purse fell and bounced off the sidewalk and onto Golden Gate, and I saw two twenty-dollar bills spin out of it, rising on currents, and I caught them, those twenties in my hand like pennants, and I'm so happy that I started running, like I don't know what, man, I'm just so happy, I mean two twenties, who would've thought? But then some guy saw me and shouted, What's he doing?, and the crowd took off after me, and man, I couldn't run fast enough. Turning a corner, I plowed right into a cop. Whoa! he said, and then all these people came up behind me shouting shit about me, and I tried to explain I'd done nothing, but it was me against all those people who said they saw me steal money from a woman's purse and some of them even said I stole the purse, and I'm going, The worst thing I did was take money from fallen purse, but I was outnumbered and the cop wasn't going to listen to me. I spent two nights in county before someone sorted things out and I got released. But by then I'd been kicked out of Hospitality Center for being absent without permission. I told my counselor what happened, but he wouldn't let me back until he spoke to the police and verified my story. I could've stayed in a shelter and waited, but I was pissed off and bummed out and pissed off some more. Maybe I was relieved too. I had a hell of a good reason to start drinking again and I took it. When my counselor saw me on the street a few weeks later, he said, Walter, you live down to peoples' expectations. He's probably right, but I did have a good three weeks.

Trust me, I tell the guy. Do what I said. Tell some war stories about when you've been drunk, talk about how you're turning your life over to your higher power and you'll be cool.

My what?

It's like God. You'll see. Just do it.

OK, he says.

No one's on the bandstand now. I feel a little chill, shiver, squint up at the sky. Blue mostly. Some haze coming in from the Richmond. I stretch and make a face at the ache in my chest. A doctor gave me pain pills but I left them in my room. He said they're good for those special kinds of headaches. Hangovers I guess is what he was getting at.

Are you married?

Yeah, the guy says. I mean when I lost my job things got kind of bad between me and my wife. We started fighting and stuff. We were doing that before, but we really got into it when I didn't have any money coming in. I mean good money, not what I was getting from Uber and Lyft. When we couldn't afford our apartment, she left me to stay with her mom. But we've been talking and texting. If I get right with a job, I think she'll come back.

And then you'll just have regular fights.

Yeah, he says.

We both laugh.

That was a good one.

Redwood lets families visit on weekends, I say.

OK, he says.

He gets up. I raise my bottle but he shakes his head.

Good luck, I tell him.

See you.

I'll be here.

He shoves his hands in his pockets and walks away. I thought maybe he'd reconsider, look back, turn around, and have a swallow, but he doesn't. I guess he really doesn't drink. Or he's stopped for now. He'll do his thing, his little scam, and I'm thinking he'll pull it off too. I hope he does. I'm for anyone who can get over with some shit. He was OK. I guess I enjoyed talking to him. Enough anyway, but he was kind of an asshole. I mean, even if he wasn't going to drink, he could've stuck around so I wouldn't be left just sitting here.

The couple I stole the wine from are holding hands, their heads tilted, touching. Too late now, but I wonder what would've happened if I'd returned their wine. You know, I could've taken it and walked a few feet behind them and put it on the ground and pretended to stumble over it or something. Shit, I'd shout, and they'd turn to me and I'd hold up the bottle and say, Someone left their bottle and I almost broke my neck. That's ours, they'd go, and I'd say, Oh, and give it to them. I could sue you, I'd say, making a joke. They'd laugh and thank me and laugh again wondering how it rolled off their blanket, and the guy'd shake my hand and she'd hug me. I'd feel every part of her and I'd hold her for as long as she'd let me, absorbing that feeling.

People around me start moving. No one's followed that last group onto the bandstand so maybe this thing is over. I take another hit from my bottle. I wonder if anyone is watching me, like they do when I go through trash looking for to-go boxes with half-eaten McDonald's and Chick-fil-A. I hate it when they stare and look sad for me. It makes me feel so alone and small. In a few months the guy who was just with me might be doing the staring. He might have a job and a place of his own again and be back with his wife. I bet he's a drinker. I wonder if he'd recognize me. I don't think so. Or maybe he would but he wouldn't want me to see him. I'd be in on his secret.

I wish I hadn't ruined the cork. I'll stopper the bottle with something and go to my room and finish it there. I'd wanted to get out, but now that I'm here I'm thinking that if I'm going to be alone, I'd rather be alone out of sight. But I'm a little buzzed and don't want to move. I close my eyes and see myself in my room nodding out. I wake up a couple of hours later, take one of those special pills and get out of bed and watch the sunset over the East Bay. In the fading light, shadows hide the fucked-up sink and cracked walls that remind me of the attic in my mom's house with its cobwebs and mildew. I take out my *Penthouse* and speak to the foldout. I tell her about the guy I met and how he's playing the system and how I hope he pulls it off, and about this young couple in love whose wine I took and how the woman reminded me of this girl I danced with like a hundred years ago in the Déjà Vu and how I can still feel her in my arms.

Miss June listens patiently, holding a bottle of wine between her tits. I'll look after you, she tells me, tapping the wine with a finger. Surf bubbles up in surging foam around her ankles, and salty ocean air puffs up her hair carelessly, thick and wild about her face. She holds a wet, blond strand with her tongue and smiles. Shhh, she goes, but I keep talking. I apologize for the cockroaches and the rats. I tell her that before inviting people over I normally sweep the floor, clean the hot plate, pots, everything, leaving not a crumb to attract bugs or pests. I won't be here long, I say. My referral will be up soon. Besides, living in a room is not me. With every breath I feel the silence. The walls hold the emptiness. I want to cry but I can't reach that far down in me for the tears.

Miss June looks concerned. Then she smiles. Her eyes beckon me with a wink. I lift her above me toward the columned skyline. The reflected glow of city lights burns gold across the evening sky, tanning her body. She puckers her lips over the bottle and blows me a kiss. I lean forward, crying. I don't know why but I'm carrying on like a child and she wipes my eyes and presses her fingers against my mouth and whispers, Shh, let's not worry about anything now.

Tom

I'm sitting at the Department of Family Services with this Iraqi guy and his family. Refugees. Fresh out of Baghdad. Arrived in San Francisco last night. I need to connect them with Social Security, SNAP benefits, and Medicaid.

Welcome to America.

His wife holds two kids and he cradles a baby girl. He points to the restroom and then himself and lifts the baby for me to hold. I shake my head no. Liability. If something were to happen while I held your baby, well, it's not going to happen.

Sorry, man, I say.

He shrugs, takes the baby with him to the men's room.

They speak no English. I need a cigarette. How do I say that? A translator at the settlement agency explained to them what we'd being doing today. He should have come with me, but, typical nonprofit, it didn't have enough staff to spare him from the office.

I tap my pack of smokes and point outside. The wife smiles, and I stand, cigarette in hand. I spread my fingers. Five minutes, I say. More smiles. Outside, the sun's reflection dances across the back windows of parked cars, and I squint, cupping a lit match in my hand.

Hey, brother, you got another one of those?

I turn and face a homeless guy I recognize right off. Little Stevie Krantz, a thin, patchy half-ass beard blotting his face like mold. Crack dealer back in the day. Walked around in a body-length mink coat no matter the weather. Hotter'n hell and there'd be Stevie in his coat, all five foot, four inches of him sweating rivers. Mister Big Man with a roll of bills in each pocket held tight with rubber bands.

Booze did him in. Just started sipping and nipping. More and more, morning, noon, and night. Next thing you know, Stevie's on Sixth Street messing himself, walking barefoot, hollering at the moon. Mink coat funky as roadkill. Booze, man, can you believe it? A fifth of this, a fifth of that. Amazing when I think about it. All that crack he dealt, and it was booze that rocked his world. Still, he was able to knock up Vernetta. Back in the day, she was as fine as she wanted to be. But in the end what she got was rank Little Stevie.

What's up, Stevie?

Tom? Hey man! I didn't know it was you!

He hugs me, raw Thunderbird breath melting my face.

Get off me!

He backs away and I give him a smoke.

Where've you been? Haven't seen you in like years, man. You're not at Fresh Start no more, Tom?

No, I say. It hasn't been that long. I left about a year ago, not quite.

Hear about your boy Michael?

I shake my head. Michael was my office manager at Fresh Start. I hired him from our shelter like most everyone else. When you're required to hire the homeless, you rely on the few Michaels of the world who don't drink, talk to themselves, or pick fights. I considered him one of the few normal people I hired. I haven't seen him for months.

He was diddling me and Vernetta's kid, man. Police called him on it.

Your kid? I can feel the love, Stevie.

Fuck that, man. Michael's running. But he can't run far. Far enough from me, anyway. Sick motherfucker diddling a three-year-old kid. I'll kill him.

I give Stevie a look like, c'mon, but he's pissed off enough to glare right back at me, his eyes shot through with the red lines like you see on road maps.

I don't know anything about that, I say.

I'm just saying so you do know. He's your boy.

I hired him. That doesn't make him my boy.

He's your boy, man.

Stevie, you've been such a standup father, I'm impressed you care.

He lurches at me and swings, his left fist just missing my face. I'm surprised at his speed, a little of the old crack-dealing Stevie not so pickled after all.

Take it easy, I say, stepping back.

I'll kill him! Stevie shouts, shadowboxing a tree thinner than him.

Where'd you hear this about Michael? I ask, feeling an old here-we-go-again weariness coming on me whenever someone tells me about one of my staff fucking up.

Streets.

Sidewalks got lips? Tell me, who told you?

I saw John. They'd started a business together.

What kind of business?

Mail.

Mail?

You on the streets, you could use their room for an address. You know how it is. Shelter's always put a time limit on how long you can have your mail sent to them. So for twenty-five bucks a month, you use Mike and John's address.

Not bad. I must have had more than a hundred guys using Fresh Start for a mailing address before I cut that shit off. Too much paper and with a staff that could not alphabetize and clients accusing us of stealing checks we couldn't find, it became my definition of hell.

John was always thinking, always laying plans for some get-rich-quick scheme. Get enough guys receiving disability or Social Security, that twenty-five bucks a month could add up. John and Michael could keep their jobs at Fresh Start, do the mail thing on the side until it took off, yeah, it could add up real good for them. Not likely, but it could if you convinced people who liked to drink and shoot up their money to part with the twenty-five-dollar fee. Good luck with that.

I resigned from Fresh Start about six months ago. I don't know, I was tired. Same people, like Little Stevie, day in day out, no change. Breaking up fights, being called all kinds of motherfucker by the same drunk who five minutes later hits you up for a dollar and who can't understand why you just eighty-sixed his ass. Staff as loopy as the clients.

Fresh Start was about the only place that would hire them, the homeless and formerly homeless. Some of them were flat-out crazy, and they knew it. I, however, had options they didn't. I could leave. I had that much going for me. When I began at Fresh Start, I wanted to save the world, but I soon learned I couldn't, and eventually I walked, quit, gave notice, whatever it's called that's what I did. It just got to be too much. Nothing ever ended. We got people into detox and then into alcohol- and drug-treatment programs, and they'd graduate and start drinking again. We placed people in housing and they would lose it. It was as if getting off the street was the equivalent of being dropped into a foreign country, much like my Iraqi family. But unlike them my clients didn't adapt—not all, but most of them didn't. I think the street changes people. Trying to get them to be who they were before they were homeless doesn't take for a lot of people, too many for me. Maybe recognizing all the pain in their lives, coming to grips with what put them out there in the first place, is just too much. I don't know, but I couldn't watch people die a slow suicide anymore. I'd had enough. Maybe I'm weak. Maybe I gave all that I could. I don't know. Maybe I should have stuck with delivering pizzas.

I'm a case manager now with International Assistance Inc., an agency that helps refugees. Mostly Iraqis, because of the war. Most, like me, have an education and job skills. They are grateful to be here. They are polite. If they drink or use, they don't do it in front of me, and they don't come to my office fucked up. Once they get settled, they find work, and I don't see them again. Ever. They're on their way. That's the way I like it. They don't come back every day like Little Stevie to show me how they are slowly killing themselves with booze or some shit.

John was my outreach worker, and if anybody was diddling anybody, I'd've thought it was him. He always brought in young women he found on the street. Hookers, runaways, slumming college graduates. He turned them over to the benefits advocate who helped them find a place to stay. Nothing wrong with it, but I wondered. Surely there were homeless men who crossed his path and needed help too. But he always found women. Young women. I told him he better not be taking them home with him. He looked shocked at the idea and denied anything. He stayed in touch with them after they found shelter or were placed in a rehab program. Follow-up, he explained. To show positive outcomes on his stats. That's legit. I was required by the state to document everything. Maybe it was a head trip, an ego thing for John, a daddy-figure thing. Still, I wondered about him. But then I wondered about all my staff. None of those gals ever complained about John, however. Never. You can't fire somebody for something you think they might be doing.

Where's John at, Stevie?

Hurley Hotel. That was their office.

Office, I mutter to myself. I give Stevie another smoke. Mike always had my back.

I know, Stevie said. He took care of Vernetta when I couldn't.

Wouldn't stop drinking is what you wouldn't do and turning her on to crack and whoring her out.

Hard to believe about Mike. Sorry I swung on you.

If I was back on the job I'd eighty-six you.

This is a public sidewalk. I can swing on whoever I want. You got another smoke?

I just gave you one. Straighten up. Look after your kid. Where is he?

Stevie shrugged.

With Vernetta's momma, I think, in Oakland.

You think? You seen Vernetta?

No. Heard she took off after this thing with Michael and hit the streets. I don't know where.

I got to go back inside.

Stevie nods, sucks on his cigarette, closing his eyes as he exhales.

So what in hell are you doing here?

Working with Iraqi refugees.

Man, what are you doing with A-rabs?

Earning a living. Later, Stevie

Later, bro.

He walks off swaying from side to side, arms out, a sailor of the streets in search of balance. I rejoin my Iraqi family. They smile, I smile back. They face forward and continue waiting for their name to be called. Patient people, for what they've been through. I give them that.

To tell you the truth, I hate like hell to be here babysitting. That's essentially what my job is. It's easy, but it's drawn out and boring. No war stories with this job. We could be here all day. I cover my face with my hands thinking and let out a long breath. Michael, Michael, Michael. Not you. Of all people, not you. I don't believe it. I don't want to.

Don't get me wrong. He wasn't a friend, really. I don't know what I'd call him. Close colleague, I guess. We went through some times together. State budget cuts, the deaths of clients and staff to addiction. It left a bond of sorts. What did I overlook about him?

I have to go, I tell the Iraqis.

They turn to me puzzled. I point outside. They smile.

Smoke? one of the kids asks stretching out the "o" sound more than he needs to, but he's learning.

Yeah, I say and stand up. Smoke and drive.

I make a motion of gripping a steering wheel. I point outside, make the driving motion again, and then point back inside.

I go. Come back.

I tell a security guard the name of the Iraqi family and ask if he would show them to a window if their name is called while I'm out. The intake workers have translators here, so I'm good on that score. The security guard's cool. Not a problem, he says. I shake his hand and leave a five-dollar bill in his palm. He smiles. No problem, no drama. It suits me most of the time, but I don't want to hold anyone's hand right now. I walk outside. I need to find John.

I'd never have noticed Michael if the copy machine hadn't jammed. But the bitch did. I was trying to print some sign-in sheets for the front desk. Something always fucked up. Running a nonprofit was hard enough without the copy machine crapping out. But when you depend on donated equipment, what you get is used and cheap and worn down. I spent more money repairing things than I would have if I bought them new. But my executive director never listened to that argument when I asked him for more money for equipment.

So there I stood staring at the copy machine's blinking red lights telling me it was in cardiac arrest.

I can fix that, sir.

I glanced at this guy looking over my shoulder. Big dude. Black, square glasses, short brown hair combed to the right side. Late thirties, maybe. Red plaid shirt tucked into his jeans, a big round belly pressing out against it. Work boots. Pleasant voice but impassive. Almost a monotone. I thought, Who called the repairman? and immediately began worrying about how much we had left in the budget for maintenance and if it would be enough to pay him.

Did we call you?

No, sir.

He smiled, just barely.

I stay in the shelter.

He stepped around me, opened a panel on the copy machine and twisted a few knobs. He yanked out the ink cartridge, pulled out a crumpled sheet of paper, and then slammed the ink cartridge back in and shut the panel. The copy machine began clicking and flashing green lights. Then it fell silent like a car with its ignition shut off. After a moment, it started humming again and the rest of the sign-in sheets began dropping into a tray.

Thanks.

No problem, sir.

I watched him take a seat in the reception area and remove a paperback book from a backpack propped against his chair. He crossed his legs and started reading.

Who is that guy? I asked my receptionist, Jay.

I don't know, he said. I've seen him around but don't know him.

How long?

A while, I think, Jay said.

The phone rings and Jay answers it.

It's a volunteer in the kitchen, Tom, Jay said. The coffee machine is broken.

Ask this Michael guy what the hell he knows about coffee machines.

The Hurley Hotel smacks up against a dilapidated convenience store. Old men, older than their years, lounge by the open door of the store, sitting on plastic milk crates and hustling crack to anyone walking by. Shriveled, even older-looking men, most of them longtime dope fiends and drunks, wander inside the store to get cash from the store owner. He receives their disability checks and serves as their payee. He takes a percentage. They buy his wine and cigarettes. They're usually broke within two weeks and he loans them money. When the next month's check arrives, he takes his percentage plus what they owe him plus interest and hands out what little remains. Naturally it doesn't carry them through the month so he loans them more money and the cycle repeats itself. They can't win. Not a bad racket. I wonder if that's what John and Mike were ultimately thinking. Use the mail drop as a way to becoming payees.

I go inside the Hurley's darkened lobby. I ask a man behind a barred window for John's room. He points upstairs.

Room 302.

Thanks.

I approach the stairs, inhale the stale air of mildewed carpet and gag. It's the kind of rank odors I've smelled in old people's homes: decay and rot and a languid, sour mugginess that suspends itself among the cobwebs replacing the air. I was used to it at one time but not now. I run up three flights with a hand over my nose, stick my head out of a hall window and suck in a deep breath. Then I knock on John's door.

Yo, John!

The door opens a hair then widens when John sees me.

Hey, Tom, he says. What are you doing here?

I haven't seen him since I left Fresh Start, but he looks the same. Short, with a gut, and the two bottom buttons of his shirt open revealing his undershirt. Gray hair brushed back off his forehead. Glasses one size too large balanced loosely on his nose.

I heard about Michael.

John lets me into a small room with two desks. Metal filing cabinets stand behind the desks. I go over to one of the desks and see a tray filled with business cards.

Michael Keys, administrator
Homeless Mail Depot Inc.

I notice small, framed photos of girls John brought into the drop-in center beside a stack of business cards with John's name and title, CEO. Little notes are scrawled across the photos. Thank you, John, I love you, John, You're the best, John. He even has one of Vernetta. He sees me looking at it.

I wasn't part of what Michael was doing, Tom.

Everyone knows you got your freak on with young girls. How young did you go?

Not that young.

Don't lie to me, John, how young did you go?

Why do you care? You're not the director anymore.

I stepped toward him. I've never kicked anyone's ass, but I'm willing to learn how on John.

222

How fucking young did you go, John?

I wasn't part of it, Tom!

How could you not know?

How could you not?

That stopped me like a red traffic light. I leaned against a desk and kind of slumped in defeat. He had me. I've been asking myself the same question. How could I not?

So what happened?

All's I know is what Jay told me, John says. Michael was at work. The police asked about him. Jay told Michael. He split. Called me from the Greyhound bus station. Said he was out of here. Gone, bing, just like that.

John slides down his chair, takes a box of business cards and throws them across the room.

So much for these, John says.

Michael fixed the coffee machine and kept the copier humming. He had other skills too. He organized the front desk, the place where everyone coming into Fresh Start had to stop and sign in. Threw away spoiled food that had been left in drawers, refilled the pen holders, and put the tokens in a plastic container. When my office assistant fell off the wagon, crack pipe in hand, I hired Michael to replace her.

I leave John's place and try to put the pieces together. What had I missed about Michael? I remember him telling me he was an army brat. Called his father "sir" long before he joined the military himself. He serviced planes. He married in his twenties. His wife got lonely living on base. North Carolina, he said it was. Fort Bragg? Anyway, she killed herself, I know he told me that. Her death sent him over the edge. He drank. He received a dishonorable discharge. He kept drinking. He hoboed around, eventually landing in San Francisco and Fresh Start.

I didn't do a background check on Michael or any of my other staff. I didn't have the budget or the time; too busy begging for money to keep my doors open to even think about doing something like that. His value to me was all I needed to know. If Michael had a record, so what? Damn near every homeless person I knew had a record. Part of the profile.

I don't doubt Michael was in the army. All that "sir" shit. Makes sense. Or at least he was an army brat. Perhaps he was married. But did she die by suicide or leave him? Was he discharged for drinking or was he thrown out because he was suspected of raping kids? Is his name really Michael?

After I hired him, he continued to spend his nights in the shelter. I told him to find his own place. He had a job, money for an apartment. He had no reason to take a cot from someone without a job. He didn't like the idea.

I wonder if he knew what would happen if he lived alone. That the shelter had not only been a place to lay his head, but a crowded, noisy place that prevented him from being alone with his desire.

Another question. I got lots of them.

I remember the day John walked Vernetta into Fresh Start. Why wouldn't I? She was the hottest thing we were ever likely to see strut through our doors. Two years ago. Man, it seems a lot longer.

Vernetta: fine, sashaying light-skinned Puerto Rican gal who made even the queens look twice. Wearing a pink dress that showed off her cleavage and trim legs. Twenty something. So hot you had a hard time making up your mind where to look. Vernetta sucked the air out of all our lungs. Even the most dazed drunks felt their heads clear and vision return, a new light in their eyes. A bottle of Thunderbird and a dime of crack had nothing on that girl.

Only Michael seemed not to notice her. He did his job with an unbroken rhythm. He asked me to sign a check request form for more bus tokens. Didn't even look up when she walked by. I signed my name and handed the check request back to him.

Thank you, sir, he said.

That day, Vernetta sat down and checked out the reception area like she owned it. We'd get people like her from time to time. Not as hot, but like her in every other way. People who didn't belong, who seemed to land from Mars and rattled our usual routine of freakouts and fights and DTs. For a moment they carried with them a fresh attitude that would give off a sense of possibility until we all calmed down and recognized them for what they were: an accident waiting to happen. Some Little Miss Thing using the gifts God gave her to get what she wanted. Booze, dope, whatever. They didn't come to Fresh Start by accident. They had just held up better than the rest.

So Vernetta started hanging with Little Stevie, who still had his groove on, although he wasn't as slick as he had been back in the day. But he still knew where to get dope even if he was too drunk to deal it himself. For a quick fuck or blowjob, Little Stevie turned Vernetta on to crack. She'd sweep into the center, zip-a-dee-doo-dah, speeding her brains out, jamming cigarettes in her mouth like firecrackers and throwing them out just as fast, talking a mile a minute. She was possessed, out of her mind. Little Stevie watched her before he passed out in a chair smiling in his sleep. Dreaming of booze and Vernetta on her knees.

It amazed me how fast she got raggedy. She stopped changing clothes. The one dress, that first one we saw her in, torn and stained. Face all droopy. Even Jay noticed. She'd look good again if she stuck her head in a tub for two hours and washed her hair, he said.

But she was feeling no pain and didn't care about how bad she smelled. I don't know when I noticed her pregnant. It just kind of dawned on me like it dawned on everybody else. Suddenly her little stick body had a bulge. I was so used to dealing with drunks, I at first thought her kidneys were going. However, that bulge got bigger and bigger and then it hit me. Oh shit, I thought, oh shit. I told her what crack would do to her baby. How it might be born blind or without an arm or a stomach. How its brain would be mush. She never sat in one place long enough to listen.

Then I stopped seeing Vernetta. She disappeared just like that. Even Little Stevie didn't know where she was. Not that he cared. He bragged about knocking her up, but that was as far as he carried his fatherly duties.

Sir, I need to talk to you, Michael said to me one morning. I looked up, budget sheets strewn across my desk. I was busy drafting reasons why the state should continue funding us.

You know Vernetta? Michael said.

Who doesn't?

She's staying with me.

I took off my glasses and pushed away from my desk.

Really.

Yes, sir. She moved in a few weeks ago. I saw her on the bus and sat with her. She's pregnant, sir.

I know.

She told me she was trying to quit using crack but had no place to stay where someone wouldn't be smoking it. I told her she could stay with me. I told her she had to attend an NA meeting twice a day and show me a note from the facilitator. Little Stevie doesn't know.

What makes you think she's not going out and lighting up when you're here?

I'd know if she was smoking again, sir. She's scared about this baby.

She should be. When's it due?

Four months.

How long has she been with you?

Three weeks. Clean so far. Hard at first.

I bet. You're putting me in a bad spot.

I know, sir.

I could fire you.

I know, sir.

I should fire you.

Michael had violated rule number one: never, I mean never, was a staff person to take a client home. All sorts of problems with that. Like exchanging a roof for sex. Even if that wasn't the case, the accusation, if made by a manipulative little dope fiend like Vernetta, would be hard to refute.

You should have taken her to a shelter.

Michael looked at me. I was full of shit and he knew it. A woman's homeless shelter wouldn't have taken Vernetta, because she was a crackhead. A battered women's shelter wouldn't want her, because she wasn't battered. A detox wouldn't want her, because she was pregnant. Liability, liability, liability. No one would have taken her. I knew that even as I spoke.

You're not touching her, are you? I'm talking even a hug.

No, sir. You can come over if you want, sir, and ask her.

She seeing a doctor?

The Tenderloin Free Clinic, sir.

How's the baby?

Good, they say. If she stays off the crack.

I look at him for a minute. He stares at the floor.

Well, sir?

It's not your fault your wife killed herself.

He doesn't say anything.

Don't do shit to make up for something that wasn't your fault.

I'm not, sir.

I'm not a shrink, but I don't have to be fucking Freud to guess that much. This isn't your kid.

I know, sir.

Find a wife and make your own kid.

I don't know where to start, sir. Vernetta sat next to me on the bus. I didn't ask for this.

We looked at each other. He took off his glasses and wiped his eyes. He looked tired.

Keep your fucking hands off her and don't say a goddamn thing to anyone else.

Yes, sir.

We never had this conversation.

Yes, sir.

I took a homeless gal home once. My first social work gig. A detox center for the homeless. Jean was thirty-seven, ten years older than me. Speed freak. Wore sandals, jeans, and T-shirts and babbled on about people thinking she looked like Janis Joplin. She was prettier than that. A cross between a deadhead and a cowgirl. She made no sense high, but I was drawn to her. I felt butterflies in my stomach when I saw her. A tingly desire. Every now and again she'd stop her speed freak chatter and look at me, and I knew she knew.

Pick me up a block from here by the park when you get off work she said one afternoon.

You have a choice, I thought as I drove my dinged-up '82 Toyota hatchback toward the park near Seventh and Howard streets. You can keep going, turn around. I didn't. I stopped. Jean sat on a swing set drawing lines in the sand, using one outstretched leg. I leaned over and opened the passenger door. Jean got in.

Ten minutes later, I parked the car outside my apartment at Masonic and Page.

I have to brush my teeth, she said when we walked into my apartment.

She went into the bathroom and I walked into my room, sat in a chair across from my bed. When she came out I said, In here. She kissed me without a word. I tasted the toothpaste mixed with cigarette breath. She dropped her pants and pulled down her panties. She was ready to do it just like that. She sat on my lap and tugged her T-shirt over her head. I looked at the scars on her stomach and her right side where she said she had burned herself rolling into a campfire.

In the morning, she asked for five dollars. I gave her twenty and a change of clothes: a pair of my jeans—a little big for her—and a plaid shirt I no longer wore. I dropped her at the park then went to work. I saw her in line at the front door waiting for us to open. She was cool. When she saw me, you'd think we'd never met.

Jean said nothing when I told her we were a one-time deal. Someone would find out. I'd lose my job by fucking a client. I suppose she expected it. She'd been around the block a few times, long enough to know there was nothing to us. When I dropped her at the park for the final time she didn't even ask for money.

I was thinking of Jean when I stopped by Michael's basement apartment in the Mission unannounced one afternoon.

Vernetta answered my knock. Her pregnancy was at a point where the T-shirt she wore barely covered her belly. But her eyes were clear, voice steady.

Tom?

Yeah. How you doing?

Real good.

What are you doing here? Michael's not at work?

I'm just checking on the situation. My staff isn't supposed to be taking in clients. Keep this visit between us, Vernetta. I'm covering Michael's ass and I want to be sure I'm not being played for a fool. May I come in?

She stepped aside. I looked around. The drawn curtains, closed windows, putrid air. A hot plate on a card table. Two chairs. A back room where the whir of a fan muffled the sounds of traffic. One lamp. Off. Everything in shadow.

Don't you want any light?

It's how Michael likes it. If he wants the lights off, they're off.

Perhaps he wanted to keep out the hot summer sun. My mother used to do that. We didn't have AC, so she'd close the curtains in the summer to keep the house cool.

I thanked Vernetta. I walked toward Sixteenth Street to catch the Muni back to work, skirting around the speed freaks hanging out in the alleys. I tried to convince myself I was making up for Jean by letting Michael take care of Vernetta. Look how good she was doing. Hell, she had a point. His place. If he wanted the lights off, he could keep them off. To each his own. Still, a part of me couldn't stop thinking it was weird.

The Hurley stands one block up from Fresh Start. I hadn't been back since my last day there one year ago. I feel an over-whelming urge now to stop by. The problem with leaving a job is that you leave part of yourself behind. The job becomes your identity. I wasn't just Tom Murray. I was Tom Murray, director of Fresh Start. Sometimes, I miss that Tom.

It feels good walking through the doors again. A man in a blue suit and tie, a bottle of air freshener by his elbow sits at the front desk.

Please stop.

I pause like a dog that had its leash yanked. I approach the desk and give him my name. I want to see the director, Deborah Brinker, I say. Miss Deborah, he corrects me. OK, Miss Deborah. No, I don't have an appointment, but she will know me. I was the director before her. He appears unimpressed. He gets on the phone and calls her office.

Jay still here?

We're not allowed to give out information on our clients. Confidentiality.

He's not a client.

Talk to Miss Deborah then.

After a brief conversation in which the front desk guy gives my name to, I presume, Miss Deborah, he hangs up and tells me to sign in. Then he points to the stairs.

You can go up now.

When I reach the top, I pause and consider what had once been my office. The door is closed. Framed university degrees hang on the wall. Miss Deborah sits behind a desk bare of anything but a computer and plastic trays filled with papers.

I knock on the door. With a sigh, she shuts off the computer, looks up, and waves me in. She reaches across the desk and shakes my hand. I wait for her to tell me to sit down. She doesn't.

Yes?

My name is Tom Murray, I say. I was the previous director.

Miss Deborah, she says. Pleasure.

I know you weren't expecting me. I just wanted to come by and tell you how sorry I am to hear about Michael and to offer my support. If there's anything I can do.

The offer hangs between us. I feel a little desperate. I want to talk about Michael. How awful I feel, how confused. But sitting and facing Miss Deborah tells me I made a mistake. I don't belong here. Not anymore.

Thank you, Mr. Murray, Miss Deborah says. It's been quite a shock. Totally unexpected.

I can imagine.

The board of directors knows about this but not our funders. I hope it doesn't go that far. Everyone understands, of course, Michael wasn't my hire.

What does that matter?

Nothing, I hope. But if this frightens funders, if they worry about the type of staff we have, I'll be forced to emphasize he wasn't my hire.

I don't say anything. I'm her excuse. She'll beat hell out of my name as long as she needs to. I don't blame her. I'd do the same thing.

Did you do a background check on Michael, Mr. Murray? Did you confirm his job histories? Michael's so-called time with the military? I did. No Michael Kelly with his birth date and Social Security number was in the army.

It's probably not his real name.

All the more reason for background checks, isn't it? And did you know Vernetta lived with him when she was pregnant? I'm sure you didn't, but why did you permit Michael to babysit for her?

What he did on his off hours . . .

He brought her baby here to work, I'm told. You must have known that much.

I don't say anything. I feel like that apostle what's-his-name when the rooster crowed every time he lied. I didn't see the harm, I want to say. Not from Michael.

I mean no disrespect, but it's a good thing you left when you did or you'd be answering a lot more questions, Miss Deborah says. I'll try to keep this from following you. You work with refugees now, right?

I just came to offer my support, I say. That's all.

Thank you.

Miss Deborah returns to her computer. I stand to leave. Then I think of Jay again.

Does Jay still work here?

He's on disability now, she says, still facing the computer.

Disability?

I had the benefits advocate enroll him in SSI. He didn't need to be here. He'd never get a job anywhere else. That does us no good. I want people who can find work and move on. Jay could barely answer the phone.

She pushes back in her chair until it rests against the wall behind her and faces me, offering a tired, even sympathetic smile that tells me she knows I think she's a bitch. She's not. She's doing what she's doing because that's what she learned in school. Comes with the degrees. She doesn't want Jay. She wants suits. She wants order. She wants to triage the Jays out of here.

You put up with a lot taking on people like Jay, Mr. Murray, she says. I'll give you that.

Vernetta had a baby boy and named him Stevie Jr. That was more credit than I'd have given his father, who never made it to the hospital. Nine damn pounds. Because Vernetta had stayed clean, the doctors thought the boy would have little to no brain damage from her use of crack. Over time they would know, but his prognosis was good.

She entered a halfway house for single moms in recovery. Michael and I used the agency van to deliver her to her new home. He hauled her things up three flights of stairs to her room. It had bay windows and a nice view of the ocean and hardwood floors that caught the sun and shined like ice.

Michael set up the baby crib. When he finished, she embraced him and sobbed. He held her like a robot and looked over her shoulder at the ocean, but nothing in his face revealed what he might be thinking. Not a blink or a tear or an expression of any kind. Just a blank stare and a stiffness to his body as he patted her back one, two, one, two and then stopped.

Pretty controlled in there, I said when we got back outside.

Military training, sir.

You should be really very proud.

I am, sir.

Don't just drop out of her life. She still needs you. Little Stevie isn't going to be any kind of dad to that kid.

No, sir, he won't. I'll come by. I told her I'd babysit.

Vernetta would bring Stevie Jr. to work from time to time and leave him with Michael while she attended an NA meeting.

After I submitted my two-week notice, I told Michael he should leave too. I knew of a job opening at Hap Street Youth Center for an office manager. After-school activities for wealthy suburban kids in Walnut Creek. Easy. No stress. Good money. Go for it, I told him. He said he would, but he never applied. To work with kids, you must agree to a background check. I hadn't thought of that before. I guess Miss Deborah had a point.

What was it like for Michael to be on that Greyhound bus after he got off the phone with John? Did he feel bad? Did he think, Another close call. I made it. I'll stop it this time. I really will. Or was his escape part of the thrill?

Sitting in his seat hunkered down, maybe a hat pulled over his face, I imagine him pretending to be asleep to avoid being noticed until he does fall asleep, only to awaken someplace else hours later. He finds a homeless shelter and sleeps among other homeless men to protect himself from himself, living below the police radar, his life resuming once more.

If Michael is caught and I'm called to testify, I would talk about the man I knew. I would stand up for that man not because I condone child abuse but because that man and I were colleagues, partners. The one guy I could say, Hey, let's have lunch, and it wasn't an act of charity. We talked about sports. We bitched about the weather. The one guy at work I could hang with because he wasn't fucking out there. I knew when I was talking to him, I was talking to him and not half a dozen personalities jockeying around in his head. He wasn't Jay. He was stiff, dull, and ordinary. He changed his clothes every day. He had all his teeth. He didn't hit me up for cash. And for a while he did a good thing by Vernetta.

Then I think, What am I doing? Look what he did. Did to me. Not just Vernetta. But Me. Me. I trusted him.

Fuck him.

I doubt the police will find Michael. If they hadn't caught him before, why would they now? He was messing with the offspring of a crackhead and a skid-row father. I'm not talking about the Kardashians here. Crack addicts and drunks. Low, low down on the priority scale.

And now Vernetta is on the street again. My kid was abused by the man who helped me, who maybe even saved my life, and who I trusted and loved, and boom, the dam broke. Violated once more, she cut loose and got herself some crack. An overwhelming desire always waiting to bust out. She needed an excuse and got a great one. And Stevie Jr., where the hell is he? Is he really with Vernetta's mother or her NA sponsor or just out there too, lost and alone?

These days, I live alone in the same apartment where I fucked Jean. I have no secrets other than her. And she was legal. Doesn't say much for me, I know, but I can leave the curtains wide open and the lights on, mirrors in place.

I hope Jean cleaned up. I hope, but I don't want to run into her and find out. I'm afraid of what I'd see, what I might be tempted to do. Like try to help her. I mean really help her this time. Guilt, man. It hangs on after all these years. I prefer to deal with people I won't see again. Like my Iraqi family. Wrap things up at the Department of Family Services this afternoon and they'll be on their way and I'll be on mine. No drama. Yes, it gets old but I can deal with old. Old is better than the alternative. If you help the same people too often, their little mindless shit will add up to either nothing or something and you've got to decide which it is and whether you can look away or not.

Me, I'd rather not know.

Acknowledgments

Thanks to the staff of Seven Stories Press, especially my editor, Dan Simon, for taking on this manuscript.

My thanks to everyone at the publications in which some of these chapters first appeared. Without you this book would not exist.

Special appreciation to David Marr, Carol Shamon, and the B Street Art Group, San Diego, for their support and interest in my work.

Thank you to Roland Sharrillo, Bruce Janssen, and Jesse Barker for critiquing early drafts of this manuscript, and to Dennis Conkin and Molly Giles for encouraging me to write. And to the memory of Thom Bartasavage and J. Walter Carson, good friends until the end.

Printed in the USA
CPSIA information can be obtained
at www.ICGtesting.com
LVHW102218250124
769457LV00001B/1